Election Day Murder

A Jackson Hole Moose's Bakery Not So Cozy Mystery #5

Sue Pepper

DIMICK LANE
PRESS

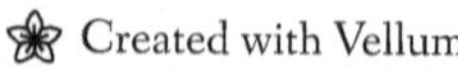 Created with Vellum

For SDB. The world is yours.

"Women belong in all places where decisions are being made."

—Ruth Bader Ginsburg, the first Jewish woman and the second
woman to serve on the Supreme Court of the United States

Content Warning

Aside from the traditional off-page murder in this book, this book also includes peril from a fire. Adultery including an age-gap relationship is a major plot point. In Chapter 23, the villain brandishes a gun and threatens to shoot two characters and themselves. As always, while a certain brown dog might get into mischief, he is happy and well at the end of the book.

Chapter One

"I love the smell of local politics in the morning!" Kendall Craig shouted, raising her voice to be heard over the eighteen-wheeler roaring by. She expertly spun the over-sized 'Paige Gates-Ortiz for Mayor' sign she held, and the trucker rewarded her with a horn toot.

Sadie Moose grimaced but waved a gloved hand at the semi driver. She blew out a puff of air and stomped her feet to warm them. It was chilly for the first Tuesday in November, even in Jackson Hole, Wyoming.

"You gotta smile!" Kendall encouraged her, a wide grin pasted on her face. She was a muscular white woman in her early twenties with close-cropped dark hair and delicate piercings along her ears, both currently shoved under a Carhartt beanie. She executed a behind-the-back sign spin move and Sadie rolled her eyes.

"Not everyone's as professional as you, Kendall," Sadie said. She was a full-figured white woman with long brown hair, freckles on her nose, and glasses. She waved her sign at a red pickup that gave her a rude gesture in return. The driver honked and thumbs-upped at the sign wavers for Paige's competitor, Wade Fisher, across the busy intersection. He was decided, then.

"That's true," Kendall said. "Back in college, I waved signs for the Original Bob's sub shop. Not Bob's Original, mind you. Much different."

"Like the difference between Alfredo's Pizza Cafe and Pizza by Alfredo?"

"Is that an *Office* reference?"

Sadie frowned. "Yes."

"You're such a millennial," Kendall sighed.

"And you're such a Gen-z-er," Sadie sighed back.

"That's why we're such great business partners," a new voice said behind them, and Kendall's eyes lit up.

"Babe!" She put the sign over her arm and spun to pick her fiancé and business partner, Claire Cabot, up in a giant hug. "You're back early!"

Claire, a petite white woman with pale blonde hair and hazel eyes, wrapped her arms around Kendall's neck and laughed as they twirled. They kissed, and Sadie's heart swelled with happiness for them. Claire had been gone on a business trip overseas for weeks, and Kendall had been lonesome without her. Of course, that meant she'd been even more attached to Sadie than normal, but considering how busy things were at the bakery and coffee kiosks they ran together, it had been okay. She'd been forced to partake in a lot of TikToks, but that was to be expected when a celebrity TikToker hung around.

"My, if that's what Paige Gates-Ortiz stands for, you can count me as a yes," a male voice said from behind Sadie. She turned and playfully swatted her friend Nash O'Conner, brewery manager at the local brewpub, where he stood. He was a tall, broad white man Sadie's age with shaggy red hair and a mountain man beard.

"Don't be gross," Sadie scolded, and Nash shrugged.

"Love is love, Moose," he said, picking up a sign from the pile and waving it. "That's all I meant."

"Plus, we're hot af," Kendall said, having come up for air. "Now, I gotta get back to sign waving, babe, but after this..." she waggled her eyebrows at a blushing Claire, who picked up her own sign.

With the addition of Claire and Nash, their numbers were greater than Wade Fisher's now, and that made Sadie happy. Paige was Sadie's lifelong best friend. A local girl, current member of the town council, licensed counselor, meditation coach, and new mom, she'd easily won her primary. She'd been highly favored to win the election early on. But land developer Wade had put his own money, of which there were deep coffers, into the race, and what little polling there was in the small town of Jackson had shown the race tightening in the last weeks.

But today, finally, was Election Day, and soon they'd know the results after weeks and weeks of plotting and worrying and planning.

Sadie's day was full of election-related activities. After sign waving through the commuting hours, she was going to vote with Paige at their local polling place, a photo opportunity and landmark occasion she didn't want to miss. Then she'd go into the bakery for a few hours before leaving to make sure the planned victory party—Sadie refused to believe it would be anything but a victory—would go off without a hitch.

Watching the sign wavers for Wade, though, they seemed just as confident. Having him win would be a major blow to the local housing movement. With land at a premium in a county dominated by a National Park, National Forest, and National Wildlife Refuge, Jackson real estate prices had always been above the average. But an influx of wealthy people looking to take advantage of lax Wyoming tax laws had led to a full-on housing crisis. As a business owner, Sadie felt the effects of the plight every day. She paid her employees a living wage and housing stipend, but it was still hard to keep staff when rents were going up and high-priced condos were replacing affordable homes.

Paige was a friend of ShelterJH, a powerful local community housing action group, and had a sound record of being on the side of the workforce with zoning and housing measures.

Wade had no prior government experience, but a lifetime of experience bulldozing homes and building unaffordable luxury condos in their place in mountain towns across the West. Name a ski community where no one could afford rent—Breckenridge, Sun Valley, Whitefish—and he'd had a hand in reducing workforce housing. Now he wanted to dismantle the progress they'd made over the years to require businesses to provide housing, increase density in neighborhoods, and change zoning laws from within, instead of fighting from the other side of the podium.

And lifelong Jackson residents were supporting him.

It galled Sadie to no end.

And after a rocky year, it had been an excellent problem to exhaust herself with. For months now, she'd been Paige's de facto campaign manager. She'd been up late every night working on the campaign, then up early at the bakery, and she'd worked herself hard enough she'd almost forgotten about *him*. And *her*.

"That lady thinks you're staring at her," Nash said, interrupting her thoughts. Thankfully.

Sadie blinked, looking away from the frowning sign waving woman. "Lost in thought," she said, waving her sign with more vigor. The traffic was slowing the closer it got to eight. They'd stay until eight-thirty, but by then school drop-off would be over, too, and the intersection would be quiet again. Another set of sign wavers was scheduled for the evening commute.

"Mmmhmm," Nash said, his full red beard quivering knowingly. "That reminds me, a certain person was at the brewery last night."

Sadie stiffened. "Who?"

"His name starts with an 'M' and rhymes with a long-bodied rodent?"

"Merritt?" Kendall said, her ears perking up at Nash's riddle. Kendall loved riddles. "He's back? Again?"

Sadie gritted her teeth. That was the last thing she wanted to hear. Today was supposed to be a *good* day. Good would win over bad. The workforce would beat a dubious developer. Her friend would prevail over a guy she didn't know that well, honestly, but who she didn't like because he had the misfortune of running against her friend. She didn't need to think about Merritt West and his mysteries.

"I don't want to hear about it, honestly," she said. She'd been working herself to the bone for weeks to avoid thinking about her childhood friend and neighbor and the short, whirlwind relationship they'd fallen in and out of a year ago.

"I do," Kendall said, and Claire echoed her. Sadie pointedly put her hands over her ears.

"Is this the first time anyone's seen him since this summer?"

"Please don't talk about that," Sadie whimpered. She didn't want to remember. The scene replayed in her head too often.

"I think so," Nash said, completely ignoring her.

"What did he say?" Kendall demanded. She'd been the one to spot Merritt when he was home in September, the one to warn Sadie they were in the same restaurant, and she should head out the back door. Sadie should've listened to her advice. She hadn't.

Nash shook his head. "I didn't talk to him, but my bar manager told me he sat at the bar around eight."

"Alone?" Kendall asked, eyebrows raised. When Merritt

had been spotted two months ago, he'd had an apparent fiancé on his arm, the glint of the diamond on her finger near-blinding.

"Alone," Nash confirmed. "He scrolled on his phone while he ate fish tacos and drank a porter."

Sadie stamped her feet, both in cold and frustration, hands still over her ears. She was thirty-three years old, and this was what Merritt West could do to her—make her act like a toddler in public. She dropped her hands and returned to sign waving, purposely ignoring the whispered conversation still going on behind her.

They were still talking when Sadie noticed one of the Fisher sign wavers, the one that had been frowning at her earlier, crossing the street to them. And she looked angry.

"You won't be so gleeful when the results are in tonight," the woman sneered as she stepped onto their crowded corner, firmly in their space. Sadie would guess she was in her seventies. She was a short white woman with a pinched look on her cold-reddened cheeks. Her demeanor didn't match the jaunty tassel on her bear-knit toque.

Sadie took a calming breath. She, too, was passionate about her candidate. "The results will be what they are," she said calmly. "But we're confident Paige will win."

The woman scoffed. "Paige Gates isn't who you think she is."

Sadie blinked, dumbfounded. "I've known Paige Gates-Ortiz," Sadie said her full name with emphasis, "since we were toddlers. I know exactly who she is."

"What are you insinuating?" Kendall asked from beside Sadie. Her friends' whispered conversation was over, their attention fully on the confrontation now.

"I don't need to insinuate anything," the woman said. "By the end of the day, everyone will know what I know, and the town will pick Wade Fisher over a liar like her!"

"What the fuck?" Nash said under his breath.

Sadie's mind raced. What could she be talking about?

"Nancy Fisher," a no-nonsense voice behind them said, and Sadie's mom, Robin Moose, pushed through the wall Sadie's friends had built behind her, standing next to Sadie. Her Paige Gates-Ortiz sign was double sided, attached to the end of a putter she held over her shoulder. She frowned at the woman. "You're making your son look bad. Get back to your corner and play nice."

Nancy's face flushed even redder, but she took a step back from them, back into the crosswalk. She held out a gloved finger and jabbed it at them. "You mark my words. This town will learn who Paige Gates really is by the end of the day. I promise that!"

"Oh, bug off," Robin said crossly. "Do you have nothing good to say about your son? You have to rag on Paige? C'mon."

"Yeah, c'mon," Kendall pitched in, and Claire punched her in the shoulder.

"Don't egg her on," she admonished.

"You don't even live here, Robin!" Nancy shouted.

Robin shrugged. She and Sadie's dad, Arlo, were snowbirds, having retired to Arizona when they passed the family bakery to Sadie. They'd spent the last summer back in Jackson, though they were planning to leave again once the election was over. "You're not hurting my feelings, Nancy. Now go wave a sign for your son and leave us alone."

Nancy looked like she wanted to scream, but the small group of sign wavers on her side of the street were calling for her to come back. She glared at Sadie once more, and turned on her heel, marching back across the street.

Right into the path of a minivan.

Chapter Two

It happened so quickly.

Nancy turned away without looking and stepped in front of the minivan.

The minivan driver was distracted, handing something into the backseat, probably to a screaming toddler.

Sadie opened her mouth to shout...

As Kendall leaped forward, dragging Nancy back by the back of her jacket, pulling her out of the way of the minivan with only a second to spare. The minivan drove on, oblivious.

"Are you okay?" Kendall asked Nancy, eyes wide, breaths coming fast.

Nancy pulled out of her grasp and looked around, aware of the eyes on them. Sadie expected her to say thank you, to gush at Kendall for saving her.

Instead, she opened her mouth and yelled, "they pushed me! The Paige Gates crew pushed me! You saw that, right?" She ran back to her friends frantically, gesturing.

Sadie cursed.

"Yikes," Claire muttered. She raised her voice. "Kendall, get out of the street before you get hit!"

Kendall turned to them, mouth agape. "But I saved her!"

"We all saw that," Sadie said. "But she's going to spin it her way."

"We should scram," Robin said, eyeing the group as they chattered at each other and sent dark glares their way. "It's about time, anyway."

"I need to call Paige," Sadie said. "And Penny." Penny Dwyer worked at the *Jackson Hole Journal* as the office manager. If anyone could head off a scandal, it was her.

"Agreed," Robin said. "Let's go. Quickly."

The group scurried away toward their vehicles. Sadie pulled her phone out of her pocket, dialing up Penny first.

"*Jackson Hole Journal*, it's a beautiful day to beat Wade Fisher, Penny speaking," Penny answered.

"Jeez Penny. Is that the appropriate way to answer your work phone? Isn't the *Journal* non-partisan?"

"I'm the only one here. Well, except for the remote workers, but they won't talk. Right, Orin? This is the circle of trust here in the bullpen, right?"

Sadie didn't hear the mumbled reply from the beleaguered Orin on the other end of the line. The *Journal* was a small operation, consisting of Penny, the Editor-in-Chief Randall, a few part-time reporters that only came in to file stories, and the printing staff. They housed remote workers for a steep fee to fill the empty desks and bring in much-needed revenue.

"Listen, this is important, Penny."

"Mmmhmm, have anything to do with this email I got from the Fisher camp about an altercation at a sign waving event?"

"They already have press out?" Sadie sputtered.

"They included a video," Penny confirmed. "Hmm...it's not a good look."

"Kendall saved her from that car!"

"And from the angle this was taken, it looks like she was pushed. Y'all are screwed."

"Why weren't any of you filming?" Sadie spun around to her friends, who looked abashed. "This is a disaster."

"Sure, sure," Penny said. "But Randall's away for a few hours, so I can keep it out of the online edition for now. Have a suitable response prepared when he calls for comment. But they're going to put the video out on social media right away. Be ready."

"Paige is going to kill us."

"Yes. She is. Good luck." Penny hung up.

Sadie stopped by her car. "Damage control meeting," she said, her friends huddling around her. "Kendall, go to the bakery and tell the table of regulars the real story. They can help through their network."

"On it, boss," Kendall said. "Are you giving me a ride?"

"Have Sully and Baxter take you," Claire offered, waving her arm at an approaching black SUV with dark window tint. "I want to go with Sadie."

Sadie opened her mouth to protest, but Claire cut her off. "I can help Paige with her statement," Claire insisted. "I don't think she'd take my crisis public relations firm's help even though I have them on retainer, but I've learned enough from them over the years." Claire's family was old East Coast money with more than one family member or associate having served time for money laundering or tax evasion. Claire was above all of that as the head of philanthropy for the family's trust, but that didn't mean she didn't occasionally get her hands dirty.

"Fine. Then you come with me to break the news." Sadie turned to her mom. "Mom, can you hit the phones with the golf girls?"

Robin nodded. "Yeah. Nancy's a pain and everyone knows it. No one's going to believe her story, anyway." She gave Sadie a quick, comforting hug and then turned toward her Subaru. "I'll keep in touch."

"Thanks mom. And Nash? Who you got for me?"

"Friend, I work in a bar. I know everyone. I got this." He swooped in to give her a half hug and then jogged to his SUV.

"I'm sorry," Kendall said dejectedly, looking at her feet.

Sadie put a hand on her shoulder and squeezed. "You have nothing to be sorry about. Without you, we'd be dealing with cops and ambulances and a perhaps-dead-opposing-candidates-mother," Sadie said. "This can be dealt with. Now, please. Opal et al.?"

"I'll have them eating out of my hand," Kendall promised, sliding into the backseat of the SUV driven by Claire's "assistant" Baxter, who also moonlighted as her bodyguard. Sadie hoped Kendall could win them over. If anyone could guide how the town reacted to this late-breaking election scandal, it would be the seven women that took up her most valuable table every morning while they drank coffee, ate scones, and steered all the town's business through their wily machinations.

Sadie watched her drive away.

"She's going to make a TikTok about this," Claire said from beside her.

"I thought about asking her not to, but what's the use? Hopefully, it will help."

"She'll do everything she can to help. You know her."

"I do," Sadie said, smiling weakly. "Now we have to go face the real boss."

Claire gulped. "I've got your back."

Sadie was going to need the backup.

* * *

Paige answered the door with wide eyes, her infant daughter, Luna, bawling on her hip.

"You're early," she said. Her strawberry blonde hair was still in overnight rollers, dark circles under her eyes. "Why are you early?" She offered Luna a pacifier, and the five-month-old batted it away, ratcheting up her screaming.

"Uhh..." Claire stepped forward and scooped up Luna, who stopped crying from the suddenness of it. "I'll take her. You two talk." She disappeared into the house.

"Why am I suddenly full of dread?" Paige asked, stepping back to let Sadie in. "Like, more dread than normal?"

"What were you in the middle of when we came?" Sadie asked, dancing around the question.

"I was going to start makeup, but Luna woke up mad, so I fed her and then she needed a diaper change..."

"P-U!" Claire cried from the nursery down the hall. "How could one small baby make so much stink?"

"I blame her father!" Paige called, and Claire laughed, then dropped her voice to talk to Luna soothingly.

"Okay," Sadie said. "Let's go do makeup and we'll talk."

Paige shrugged and made her way into the bedroom she shared with her husband, lawyer Mateo, then to the attached bathroom. She plopped down in her chair in front of the vanity. "My phone has made a lot of buzzing sounds in the last ten minutes, and I haven't looked at it, so you might as well just tell me now."

Sadie leaned against the counter, watching her friend start her makeup. Paige was a white woman, slim, with shoulder length hair, brown eyes, an earnest, oval face, and a pale complexion. She was fierce, a fighter, and her best friend. The dark circles under her eyes made Sadie's heart hurt. Between the sleeplessness of life with a newborn and seemingly endless campaign, the last few months had been hard on her. And she was about to make it harder.

"Do you remember when you caught Jeremy Holden kissing a random blonde under the bleachers when we were supposed to be exclusive?" Paige asked suddenly.

Sadie met her eyes in the mirror. "Uh...yes?"

"And remember that you worried over telling me for so long you threw up during sixth period biology?"

They'd also been dissecting frogs, but Sadie grimaced. She remembered. "Oh. Yes?"

"We don't have time for that kind of worrying today. Spill it."

Sadie took a deep breath. "At sign waving this morning Wade Fisher's mom started a verbal altercation with us and she almost got hit by a car. But Kendall saved her! But she's claiming that Kendall pushed her. They've apparently posted the video on social media."

A muscle clenched in Paige's jaw, but otherwise her face didn't change, her hand continuing to steadily apply brow pencil.

After a moment, Sadie cleared her throat. "You heard me, right?"

"I'm thinking," Paige said tersely.

Sadie waited, trying not to jiggle her leg or worry her lip. She tried to be the picture of serenity...and failed.

When Paige had finished her makeup, shaken out her curls, and taken a deep, calming breath, she stood. "So, Kendall is a hero. We'll focus on that."

"Perfect plan," Claire said, sweeping into the room with Luna in her arms. "I presumed she was supposed to wear this tiny pantsuit?" She held the baby out so they could see her. Luna wore a navy-blue double-breasted jacket with matching trousers and Mary Janes, a miniature of Paige's outfit hanging on the back of the bathroom door. A red, white, and blue bow in her downy black hair finished off the look.

"Awwwwwwww," Sadie crooned, holding out her arms to take Luna. "Come to Auntie. Look at you!"

"That's our voting outfit," Paige confirmed, standing and shooing them out the door. "Let me change. Thanks for getting her ready. Mateo should be home in a minute."

"She seems fine?" Claire whispered when the door closed.

Sadie pulled a face. "I think she's wound pretty tight, but she's holding it together." Luna grunted in agreement, a tiny fist in her mouth. She was teething and always had something in her mouth...a fist, a toy, a phone, keys. She wasn't picky.

They tromped into the living room to wait for Paige. Sadie plopped Luna in the bouncer to entertain herself, then busied herself gathering the stuff they'd need for the baby gear bag. A couple of bottles from the cabinet. Formula. Water. Burp cloths. The changing pouch needed wipes, so she dug around in the hall cabinet, knocking over a pink walkie talkie and a stack of puzzles, looking for a new one.

Claire pulled out her phone and tapped on it. After a moment, she spoke. "How does this sound? 'The Gates-Ortiz campaign is aware of a video on social media showing one of their volunteers saving a woman from the path of an oncoming vehicle this morning. We are grateful to the volunteer for her quick thinking and action, and grateful no one from either campaign was hurt. We encourage all volunteers to be aware of their surroundings and are reevaluating our afternoon sign waving events.'"

"Perfect," Paige said as she entered. "Text it to me and I'll post it."

"Done," Claire said, her phone making a whooshing sound.

Sadie took in Paige's full look and whistled. She looked professional, confident, and...mayoral. "Looks like the new mayor!" She gave her a hug and felt the tension in Paige's shoulders when she did so. "You've absolutely got this," she whispered in her ear.

"I need you to do the thing," Paige said quietly when Sadie pulled away. Sadie examined her. She was pale beneath her makeup.

"The thing?" Claire asked, bewildered.

"Oh, okay!" Sadie said, thinking fast. "Uh...remember when Elizabeth Warren ran for President and she'd say in her speeches, 'I'm Elizabeth Warren, and I'm running for President, because that's what girls do?' And she'd do the pinky promise with all the little girls she met on the campaign trail?"

Paige nodded, squaring her shoulders. "Yes, okay, more."

Claire narrowed her eyes at them. "I think I get it. Let me try. Remember in 2019 when AOC got sworn in and she wore white in honor of suffragettes?"

"Good one," Sadie whispered to her. "And remember when they finally called the election in 2020 and Kamala Harris was on a jog and they posted that video of her saying, 'we did it, Joe'?"

Paige was bouncing on her toes now, color in her cheeks. "Yes! More!"

Mateo came through the door at that moment. After a pause, he said, "remember when you won the election for mayor of Jackson by an absolute mile, leaving stinky Wade Fisher in the dust, and your election put the town on a sustainable path for the workforce?"

"Ooooooh," Sadie and Claire said in unison, and Paige grinned.

"That'll do it," she said, chin held high. "Now let's go vote."

On the way out the door, Paige leaned into Sadie. "What was the altercation about, anyway? You never said."

"Oh. Nancy Fisher was going on about how she had some

sort of info about you that would change the way we thought of you. What a bullshitter." Sadie glanced at Paige, who didn't immediately reply. "Right?"

"Yeah, of course," Paige said, shrugging it off. "There's nothing like that out there. It's all fine."

But as they climbed into their vehicles to head to the polling place, Sadie couldn't help but replay the moment in her mind. Had Paige swallowed hard when she said that? Something had seemed off. But Sadie knew all of Paige's secrets, and none of them could change how she saw her...right?

Chapter Three

Their polling place was at the fairgrounds, located right in the center of town. Sadie had shaken off any unease she felt by the time she and Claire parked and exited the car. They waited in the cold for Paige, Mateo, and Luna, who sat in their car for what seemed like too long.

"What are they doing?" Claire asked, peering in.

"It looks like Mateo's giving her a pep talk," Sadie said. "She's nervous."

"Even after the thing? I thought we did pretty good."

Sadie nodded absently. "I wish I knew what Nancy Fisher meant earlier."

"About info on Paige? I can't imagine she was telling the truth."

"But even a lie could hurt us," Sadie insisted. "What a dirty under-handed trick."

"I'll monitor the Internet," Claire promised. "Even a whiff of scandal and I'll let you know right away."

The Gates-Ortiz family finally joined them, Luna in Paige's arms. Paige's eyes were red.

"Oh, babe," Sadie cried. "Are you okay? Were you crying?"

Paige sniffled. "It's Mateo's fault."

Sadie glared at him, and he held his hands up. "I gave her a gift. I didn't think it would make her cry."

Paige reached into the inside pocket of her coat, withdrawing a fancy pen. She held it up for Sadie to read the inscription.

"Madame Mayor," Sadie read. She felt her own eyes prickle. "Awww, Mateo."

"I was going to give it to her tomorrow, after the results were final," Mateo said. "But I'm so confident in her, I decided she should use it to vote for herself."

"That's the sweetest thing," Claire said, wiping her eyes.

"I told you it was his fault," Paige said, blowing her nose in her handkerchief. She put the hanky and the pen back in her coat pocket. "Now. We need to go. It's cold out here!"

The group strode toward the fairgrounds entrance, past the big VOTE HERE signboard. There wasn't a line, which Sadie wouldn't expect so early in the day, so they went right inside. A familiar face greeted them in the vestibule.

"Kamari, I didn't know you were working the polls," Sadie said, surprised. Kamari Robinson was one of her baristas, as well as Kendall's best friend and former roommate. She lived with one of Sadie's other employees, Sage Wallace, in Sadie's basement.

Kamari looked at them critically over her glasses. She was a tall, athletic Black woman in her early twenties. Aside from her bakery job, she was an up and coming freeride skiing star with a ski film coming out in a couple weeks. "I'm doing my civic duty," she said to Sadie. She narrowed her eyes at Paige. "I don't have to warn *y'all* about electioneering, do I?" she asked.

Paige frowned. "Of course not. None of us are wearing pins or anything. We're just here to vote."

"I had to tell Wade Fisher and his wife to stop glad-handing in the line," Kamari said, annoyance in her tone. "Apparently he thought he could come in here and try to influence votes."

"Yikes," Sadie said. "I'm going to get a photo of the family voting. Did you notice the matching pantsuits? But otherwise, we'll be in and out."

Kamari softened a little when Paige took off her and Luna's coats, tucking them under her arm to reveal the outfits. "Okay, y'all are cute. Now go get in line."

"Should we go outside and wait for Wade to leave?" Paige asked Sadie under her breath. "I don't want to interact with him if I can avoid it."

"Too late," Claire said quietly, eyes behind them. Loudly, she said, "Mr. Fisher, good morning."

Paige pulled a face, but smoothed it out, turning to greet her opponent. "Wade, Madison, hello. Happy Election Day!"

Wade was a handsome white man in his mid-fifties. He had an expensive haircut and blue eyes and wore a suit that screamed he watched the show *Yellowstone* and it influenced his entire personality. His wife, Madison, was on his arm. She was close to twenty years his junior, a former Miss Arizona, a white woman with blonde hair, big white teeth, and a lot of eye makeup. She looked bored and cold, with her red Patagonia puffy coat zipped to her neck and gloves still on.

"Well, it started off rough," Wade said sorrowfully. Paige stiffened. Then he lifted his head, a sly grin on his face. "But it will be a happy Election Day when I take home the W," he said, grinning. He held out his hand to shake Paige's, then Mateo's, and then Luna's. Or at least he tried to shake Luna's hand. She knocked it away instead, grunting. "She's got spunk like her mama!" Wade said, winking at Mateo, who grimaced.

"There's no loitering after voting," Kamari broke in, her tone firm. "Vote, then leave."

"Oh, we haven't voted yet," Wade said. "The missus had to

use the powder room, so we got out of line and we're about to go back in."

"Great," Kamari said. "Then please do so." She was losing her patience.

"Let's all go," Sadie said. The door behind them opened. "We don't want to cause a pile up here." She opened her arms, gesturing that they should move.

Wade and Madison strode forward like they were worried Paige would race them, but Paige held back. "I think we should go outside and wait," she said firmly. "It's not appropriate for us to be in there together."

"It could be perceived as a weakness," Claire said carefully. "If you leave and he tells people…"

Paige groaned. "I can't wait for this to be over," she murmured. "Okay. Let's go. Eyes front, avoid all contact with them. There's already enough controversy today."

They filed into the large exhibit hall. Tables staffed by election judges spanned the room, each with a set of letters on them. Behind them, the line to vote in the curtained voting booths around the outer edge of the building snaked around. There was an excited din of low voices, and heads turned their way as they entered.

Paige hummed a popular line from *Speak Now* by Taylor Swift and Sadie gave her shoulder a squeeze.

"You got this. RBG's dissent in Bush v. Gore."

"The 'I dissent' ruling. Good shit right here," Paige said. "See you on the other side?"

They split up by last name. Sadie noticed with trepidation that Wade and Paige were in the same letter group. As she waited in line, she watched them. He leaned forward to say something in Paige's ear, and she stiffened and stepped away. What had he said to her? Something about this morning? Something…about whatever Nancy had threatened Paige with?

"Sadie Moose, pay attention," a stern voice said, and Sadie snapped back to the current moment, meeting the eyes of Gretchen Whitehouse, one of her table of regulars.

"Gretchen," Sadie said, stepping forward. "I forgot you worked the polls."

"Every year since the kids started school," Gretchen said, perusing the spreadsheet in front of her. "ID please?"

Sadie pulled her wallet out of her pocket, brandishing her driver's license. Like Gretchen hadn't known her since she was wandering around the bakery in pigtails. But rules were rules, and in Wyoming, you had to show ID to vote.

Gretchen scrutinized it carefully. She was a white woman, nearing seventy, who always had a romance novel on her person. Sadie didn't see one shoved into the pockets of her barn coat, but she would bet anything there was at least one if not multiple in a tote bag at her feet. After studying her ID like a bouncer at a club recently busted by the cops, she handed it back. "Here's your ballot. Proceed to a booth when one opens. When you're done, hand it to the ballot counters. They'll give you a receipt, and a sticker."

"I love stickers," Sadie said absently. It had gotten quieter in the room. Hushed. The vibe was...different. "All good here today, Gretchen?"

Gretchen frowned. "Except for the fact we have both mayoral candidates here at the same time and one of them already got in trouble for electioneering? I had to tell that Madison Fisher she couldn't wear a campaign t-shirt to the polling place, and she *rolled her eyes at me* when she zipped her coat up over it. My stars, can you believe it? Anyway, you need to move along before I get backed up."

"Sorry, sorry." Sadie took her ballot and proceeded to the line. The Gates-Ortiz family had moved quicker than her and were several voters ahead. Wade Fisher must have slow walked it though, because he and Madison ended up behind her. She wasn't sure where Claire was. Was Claire even registered to vote in the county?

Sadie tried not to listen to Wade and Madison's whispers, but she overheard enough of the conversation to understand Madison was *not happy* with Wade. It sounded like normal couple bickering. Before she could eavesdrop more to confirm, the line moved forward, and everyone including Wade and Madison moved into empty booths to vote.

The booths were spread a foot apart and were just large enough to step in and close the curtain. Sadie took a deep breath as she stepped in and laid her ballot out. She didn't have a special pen, so she'd use the one provided. With joy in her heart and hope in her veins, she filled in the bubbles for the open federal and state seats, then came to the mayoral choice.

Paige Gates-Ortiz or Wade Fisher.

In the easiest decision she'd ever made in her life, she put her pen on the paper and began filling in the bubble.

And then the fire alarm blared.

* * *

And it wasn't only an alarm. Sadie thought she smelled smoke.

Shit.

What should she do? Take her ballot? Finish it quickly?

A loud voice decided for her. "Everyone evacuate to your nearest exit now. Leave everything behind." There was a screeching sound, and then the voice repeated the statement over a megaphone.

Shoes pounded on the floor as people headed for the exits. She slipped out of her booth and gasped. Smoke filled the large hall. The source wasn't obvious. She saw no flame, but the smoke was only getting thicker. She looked around frantically for her friends.

"Mateo!" He was to her left, Luna's face turned into his jacket to protect her lungs. He looked frantic.

"Where's Paige?" she called.

"I don't know! She was right here, and now she's gone!" He coughed, and Sadie put her arm over her face, feeling her own lungs fill with smoke.

"You go out with Luna. I'll look quickly and then meet you outside," Sadie promised.

Mateo looked like he wanted to protest, but with his baby in his arms, he had no choice but to listen to her. He hurried away, disappearing into the choking smoke out the north doors.

Sadie turned back to the voting booths, but the smoke was so thick she couldn't see across the room. Where would Paige have gone? Sirens wailed outside. This wasn't smart. She should go out and let the firefighters come in to sweep the building.

She decided she'd head toward the exit opposite of where Mateo had gone, to the south doors. He hadn't found her on the way out, or he would've yelled for her, so maybe Paige was that direction. Had she fallen? Hurt herself? Her left ankle had a tendency to roll from a tennis injury in eighth grade. But wouldn't she be yelling, calling for help?

It was eerily silent in the building, except for the growing crackling of flames. Was Sadie the last one inside?

She hurried toward the exit, holding her jacket up over her mouth and nose and ducking low to stay out of the smoke. Sadie was halfway to the exit, or at least best guess halfway to the exit, when she heard a yell. She stopped, cocking her ear in that direction.

"Paige?" She called, then coughed, having inhaled too much smoke. "Paige, is that you?"

She heard footsteps running in the opposite direction.

Flame flared for the first time near the vestibule where they'd come in. That was it. She needed to get out now, before her trying to help someone else ended up getting her killed.

She put her head down and rushed forward. She had to be almost there.

And then she tripped, sprawling headlong onto the hard concrete floor.

"Ouch!" Sadie cried, pain shooting through her left arm, which she'd—stupidly, she thought—caught herself with. She rolled onto her back, clutching her wrist. It really hurt. Like, maybe she'd broken something hurt. She opened her eyes. Her wrist was hanging at an unnatural angle. Oh no. And she couldn't see anything above her more than a foot. Black smoke choked the air, and she could feel the heat of flames on her face. She had to get out of there. But what had she tripped over?

Tears spilling from her eyes from the pain, from the fear, from the unknown, Sadie pulled herself to her feet, cursing the whole time. She looked around and froze.

She knew what she'd tripped over now.

It was a man's leg encased in an expensive Western-cut suit and overpriced ostrich-leather boot. Two of them. Connected, Sadie saw, as she swayed closer, bile rising in her throat, to the torso and head of Wade Fisher.

His eyes were wide open, staring at the ceiling, his cowboy hat knocked aside and dribbled with blood.

Blood, from the wound on his neck.

Where he'd been stabbed.

With a pen.

Chapter Four

Sadie stumbled out of the building and into the fresh, cold air. Choking on her sobs, gasping, clutching her injured wrist across her chest, she ran right into the path of a firefighter in full gear, including an SCBA mask. One look at her, and he turned around, calling for a medic.

"Police," Sadie said hoarsely. "We need the police."

"What?" The firefighter asked through his mask, one arm wrapping around her to help her stand.

"Dead," Sadie said. "He's dead."

The man's eyes widened. "Who, ma'am?"

Sadie's eyes flitted about the crowd growing around her, despite the efforts of the firefighters and arriving law enforcement to keep them back. Her eyes met Madison Fisher's. She was sobbing, her phone to her ear. Soot covered her Fisher for Mayor shirt. Sadie could make out the words she was saying repeatedly. "Pick up, pick up!" She was calling Wade.

And he wouldn't be answering. Sadie's heart broke for her.

She turned away from the crowd. "Wade Fisher. He's dead in there. Murdered, I think."

"Oh shit," the firefighter exclaimed. "Shit!"

And then the paramedics were there, leading her away, and Claire was suddenly by her side. She looked no worse for wear, where Sadie was a smoky, sobbing, coughing, injured mess.

"Paige?" Sadie asked as they hustled her toward an ambulance parked nearby.

"Safe," Claire said. "When you came out, I told them they should leave. They needed to take care of Luna, and Paige needs to check with the county on their contingency plans."

Right. The election.

But one of the candidates was dead.

As Sadie was settled into the back of the ambulance, oxygen immediately offered to her, she remembered something.

Something about the pen.

She'd seen it before.

And then she passed out.

* * *

When Sadie came to, she was no longer in an ambulance. Was she home? She opened her eyes. They felt swollen, from the smoke, from the tears. Her vision was blurry, and she blinked to clear it.

She recognized the ceiling tiles.

Well, damn.

She was in the hospital.

She sighed. She hated the hospital. A comforting hand came down to cover hers, and her eyes flitted around to see whose it was.

The smiling face of Hector Sanchez, her favorite nurse, greeted her.

"You're not wearing Garfield today," Sadie croaked, eyeing his scrubs. "Who's the blue dog?"

"Bluey! You don't known *Bluey*? You need to watch on

Disney Plus," he said. "My daughter is obsessed. She's legit getting an Australian accent."

None of that made any sense to her, and Hector must have noticed. "Feeling pretty poorly, aren't you, *chica*," he said. He scanned the screens that showed her vitals. "You're doing okay though. Need oxygen, some fluids. We've got pain meds going in, too. We'll take you down for an x-ray on that wrist soon."

At the mention of her wrist, she remembered. Falling. Over the body. Wade Fisher's body! Had she told anyone? Her scrambled brain struggled to remember. The firefighter. She'd told him.

"You don't need to worry, Sadie," Hector said soothingly. "We only brought in a few victims for smoke inhalation. I hear they're getting the fire under control." He didn't mention the body. But would he know? And there was something important she needed to remember.

"Paige!" Sadie cried, trying to sit up. The motion jostled her hurt wrist, and she cried out in pain.

"Woah, woah," Hector said, gently restraining her back into the bed. "You can't move around like that. And Paige is fine, as far as I know. She's not here, at least?"

"I need to talk to her."

Hector must have heard the fear in her voice, because instead of more soothing words, he arched an eyebrow. "What have you gotten yourself into this time, Sadie?" He asked. "Is your phone in your coat?" He dug through the plastic bag containing her things, which was when Sadie realized she was in a hospital gown and nothing else. Man. She'd really been through it, hadn't she? They wouldn't let her out of here anytime soon.

"Phone," Hector said, holding it up. "You have thirty-seven missed phone calls."

Sadie pulled a face. "That reminds me. Did anyone come with me to the hospital?"

"No," Hector shook his head. "Paramedic said a little blonde wanted to come, but she wasn't family, so they couldn't let her. I'm sure your crew will show up any minute." He shuddered, then brightened. "I hope your mom brings cookies." His communicator beeped, and he pulled it to his ear to listen.

"I have to go to another room," he announced. He put her phone in her lap. "Don't make me regret giving this to you, okay?"

Sadie promised, and he left. Her head felt lightweight, like that time she'd gotten a secondhand high at a Brandi Carlile concert. The pain meds must be working. She needed to call Paige now, before she couldn't tell her what needed to be said.

Luckily, she'd injured her left arm. She examined it, the odd angle of her wrist. Damn, was it really broken? How was a baker supposed to knead dough with one hand? Pie season was just around the corner, and then sugar cookie season. She'd be worthless. She carefully picked up her phone, unlocking it and going to the missed calls. Her parents had called her a dozen times, and Paige and Mateo made up the other calls. She had missed texts, too, from Kendall, Claire, and Kamari, as well as others. If she hadn't felt so poorly, she would've taken a moment to bask in the warmth of the obvious care and concern of her friends. But she felt horrible, so she didn't have time for that.

She dialed Paige. She answered immediately.

"Sadie! Are you okay?"

Sadie's tongue felt thick. "I'm in the hospital, but I think I'll be okay," she said.

"Ugh, I saw you come out. I should have stayed! But Luna was cold and coughing, and we were so worried about her, and Claire said she would take care of you."

"It's okay," Sadie said. "Listen—"

"It's not okay, I'm a terrible friend!"

Sadie groaned. She needed Paige to listen. "Paige, stop. Listen to me for a minute."

Paige quieted.

"Is Mateo with you?"

"Yes..."

Sadie took a deep breath. "When I was leaving the hall, I tripped..."

"Okay?"

"Over Wade Fisher. He's dead."

Silence.

"Did you hear me?"

"I'm...what? How is that possible, Sadie? I..." Paige's voice trailed off.

"Paige?"

"The police are here," Mateo said in the background. "Why are the police here?"

Things were spiraling too quickly, and Sadie's head was getting mushier and mushier. She had to tell Paige the last thing.

"Listen to me. Don't tell them anything. I saw...I saw how he'd been killed. And it was with your pen."

The sound Paige let out was unlike anything she'd ever heard come from her friend. And she'd been in the room supporting her when she gave birth to Luna. It was pain, and fear, and shock. There was a rustling sound, and then Mateo came on the line.

"What's going on? Tell me quickly." Mateo's normally friendly voice was clipped. While he generally dealt with immigration and family law, he'd done criminal work before, including representing Sadie in a case she'd been accused in last year.

"Wade Fisher was murdered, and I saw Paige's pen in his neck."

Sadie heard a knock on their door. A loud one. An assertive one. A "we've come to take you in" sort of knock.

"*Mierda*," Mateo cursed. "We've gotta go."

And he hung up.

Sadie felt tears prick at her already-swollen eyes. How had the day come to this? She glanced at her phone again. It was only ten-thirty in the morning, and the day had gone from promising, inspiring...to a tragedy.

Her phone vibrated in her hand, and she looked down at it. Mom.

She lifted the phone to her ear, tears in her voice. "Mommy?"

"Oh, baby," Robin said. "I'm on my way. Daddy's headed to the bakery to check in, then he'll come too."

"I'm doing okay," Sadie said, trying to sound strong. "I just hurt my wrist, but Mama, Paige..."

"Shush," Robin soothed. "You can tell me all about it when I get there."

* * *

The next face Sadie saw when she next opened her eyes wasn't her mother, though.

"We have to stop meeting like this," Detective Will Nolan said, the joke not quite meeting his piercing blue eyes. He was a tall, clean-shaven white man with sharp, interesting features that could even be handsome on the rare occasion he smiled.

Sadie cleared her throat, which felt raw. "In the hospital?"

"Because of a murder investigation," Will clarified.

Sadie closed her eyes. "I'm going back to sleep."

"No luck," he said. "I need to talk to you. Pretty urgently."

"I'm on meds," Sadie said. "And my lawyer's not present. You know I don't talk without a lawyer."

"Your lawyer's pretty busy at the moment," Will said.

Sadie's eyes snapped open. "I don't like your tone."

Will shrugged his shoulders. "Just doing my job. Keeping it professional. You know."

Which is what she'd asked him to do. Last summer, the tenuous friendship they'd developed over the course of a year cooperating on cases had blossomed into something else. A passionate kiss, a surprising rapport, a very nice date...that had ended abruptly when Sadie had spotted Merritt with his fiancé on his arm. Afterward, she'd been despondent. She'd tried one more date with Will, but the spark had been gone. So, she'd asked for them to keep things professional from then on. And he'd answered by practically disappearing from her life. No more conversation in the bakery line because he didn't come in for his normal shot in the dark and scone anymore. It had been one more thing Sadie had been trying to forget by throwing herself into the campaign these last few months.

"I'm not talking."

"You won't give a statement? I have a statement from the firefighter that helped you out of the building. I know what you told him. I want you to tell me in your own words."

"And I'm not dumb." She wanted to explain why. That she knew she was the last person to see Wade Fisher and she could be a suspect, too. But she wouldn't even say that. "I will not speak without a lawyer present."

"She sounds pretty firm on that, officer," Hector said, coming through the door. "I'll ask you to leave now. I'm taking her down for an X-ray for that arm. And then we're going to get her cleaned up."

Sadie wrinkled her nose. She smelled like the smoke, a chemical char. She had so many questions. At one time, she would've been able to ask them of Will. But not anymore. That was behind them. "I'll have my lawyer make an appointment to make a statement," Sadie said. "When I'm well enough."

"I could charge you with impeding an investigation," Will said, his face stormy.

"You could," Sadie said as Hector pushed her out the door in her bed. "But you won't."

As Hector pushed her down the hall, leaving Will behind, he leaned in close. "That man can't decide if he wants to kill you or kiss you."

Sadie sighed. "Kissing is off the table. I can't find the line between cop and friend, much less boyfriend, with him. It's not happening for me."

Hector laughed. "With the company you keep and the situations you find yourself in? Girl, I don't blame you. You need to find a lawyer. Or a billionaire who can buy your way out of these messes."

Sadie laughed, even though it hurt to do so.

"Naw," she said, her head swimming from the motion of the bed. "I'm a lone wolf. Lone moose." She giggled. "A-lone moose."

"You're high as a kite," Hector said, amusement in his voice. "I'm turning down your drip."

"You're no fun," Sadie pouted.

"Nope," Hector agreed. "And you're not going to like this part, either."

Chapter Five

Hector was right. She didn't enjoy the X-ray, which required her arm to be moved around in ways that hurt a heck of a lot. And she didn't enjoy being assisted in the shower, which she'd steadfastly insisted on instead of the sponge bath Hector said she was required to get. But when she was in a clean gown on clean bedding and in her room again, she felt a little better. Hector had been true to his word and turned her pain medication drip down, so her head wasn't swimming as much. And her mom was there.

To Hector's delight, she'd brought cookies.

When they were alone, Sadie told her what happened.

Robin, always matter of fact, listened intently, then sat back in her chair, considering.

"Mateo has Paige covered. You need to stop worrying about her."

"What about Luna?"

"I'm sure Paige's mom can take care of her. I'll text though, to check in. This will all work out. You and I both know Paige didn't do it."

"I know. And I didn't."

"I know," Robin said, a soft smile on her face. "But we need to get you a new lawyer. I'll have dad make some calls."

"What does this mean, mom? For the town? For the election?"

"I have no idea," Robin sighed. "We've been early voting for weeks, so a lot of votes are already in. Do they only tally what they have? There has to be some sort of protocol for it. They'll figure it out. That's not your worry either."

"But what if Wade wins?"

"Another thing you can't worry about right now, babe," Robin said, patting her non-splinted hand.

The doctor came in. His news wasn't great. Sadie had a distal radius fracture. It was a clean break and, after straightening—which Sadie didn't like the sound of at all—she'd be in a splint for a few days until they checked the bones again on an X-ray. Then they'd cast it. No surgery, probably, which was good news.

"And at least it's your left!" The doctor said cheerfully.

"A baker needs two hands," Robin said, and the doctor's face fell. "And the smoke inhalation?"

"Irritated lungs, but no permanent damage. We'll continue to give oxygen, but I suspect she'll be released tomorrow."

Tomorrow. A whole night in the hospital, wondering what was happening outside the walls. Was the news about Wade out yet?

Robin plied the doctor with a cookie. He promised to be back shortly to do the straightening and splinting, but she was to rest in the meantime.

Sadie tried. She really did. But with the oxygen flowing and the pain meds turned down, she felt wide awake. Her mind was spinning, and not in a fun way.

"What happened this morning with the golf girls?" she asked, finally giving up.

Robin pursed her lips, looking at her phone absently. "They all agreed Nancy was full of it."

"Seems like the least of our worries now," Sadie sighed.

Robin was silent.

"Mom?"

Robin held her phone out for Sadie to read a news headline. Her stomach dropped.

MAYORAL CANDIDATE DEAD, RIVAL BEING QUESTIONED

And it wasn't from the *Journal*.

It was from a twenty-four-hour cable channel.

Jackson Hole, population under 11,000, had hit the national news.

* * *

Arm straightened and splinted, oxygen levels normalized, and a good amount of wheedling and promises later, Sadie rolled out of the hospital in a wheelchair. It'd been three hours. Yes, they'd wanted to keep her overnight...but they couldn't keep her if she didn't want to stay. Sadie had a feeling Hector pulled some strings to get her released so she didn't have to sign the scary hospital forms saying she was leaving without their consent. She'd owe him dozens of cookies. A price she was willing to pay.

Because Sadie couldn't stay in the hospital.

Paige was in police custody for Wade's murder. Not arrested. Not yet at least, but being held for questioning. It was unthinkable. Unimaginable! On the day that was supposed to be her greatest triumph.

And Sadie wouldn't let it stand.

She didn't care that her left arm was immobilized and painful, didn't care that she didn't even know where to begin.

She wouldn't let Paige take the blame for Wade's death. If she had to, she'd find the murderer herself.

She'd gone over the events at the polling place innumerable times in her head.

They'd gone into the booths.

After a minute, the fire alarm had gone off, and the room had filled with smoke.

She'd left the booth to find most people already rushing off. She'd seen Mateo and Luna, who were looking for Paige. She'd sent them out the closest door and decided she'd look for Paige going out the other door. But on the way, she'd tripped and fallen over Wade, shortly after hearing a yell and footsteps. The whole crime had to have happened in mere minutes. How had someone gotten a hold of Paige's pen? How had that been enough to kill a strong, robust man like Wade? Why had Paige disappeared in the first place? How had the fire started? There were so many questions unanswered.

Robin took Sadie home. Sadie let herself be shuffled inside, then helped in the shower to get the smell of smoke out of her hair for good, then put into her bed with her arm propped up. She promised she'd stay in bed, and sleep, and not let the chaos happening in town between a murder and botched election keep her up. And she really did try. She tried for a full ten minutes. Just long enough for her mom to leave the house, cross the alley, and go into her own house. Plus a few extra minutes to make sure she wasn't watching.

And then she pulled loose pants on under her oversized sleep shirt, wincing at the pain, put on shoes, slung a coat over her shoulders, and snuck out the front door.

She had investigating to do.

* * *

The county had stood up an emergency polling place at the city clerk's office, where they did early voting. They'd sent the election judges scheduled to work the fairgrounds polling place to the outlying county voting locations to handle a surge in voters.

So, first on Sadie's list of things to do was to vote, because she'd been very rudely prevented from doing so earlier. The line outside the city clerk's office was around the block when Sadie joined it, but it moved quickly. While she waited, she tuned into the conversations going on around her.

"Murdered!"

"There's no way Paige…"

"I could see Paige doing it…"

"He deserved it…"

The voices swam around her, in turn angering and soothing her. Or was that her head, still swimming from the pain medication?

"You're not supposed to be out of bed," said a voice right next to her, and Sadie snapped to attention. It was Kendall, looking sly.

"Don't tell on me?"

"Oh, I won't," Kendall promised, inching into the line with an apologetic look at everyone she was cutting in front of.

"How'd you find me, anyway?"

"I went to your house for my scheduled check-in, and you weren't there, so I used my phone to find yours."

They'd agreed that connection was only for emergencies, but Sadie supposed this counted. "Wait, scheduled check-in?"

Kendall showed her a text on her phone. "Your mom has someone scheduled every hour until ten tonight, so if you plan to stay out, you'll need to bribe Gavin next."

"That's easy enough," Sadie sighed, marveling at her mom's efficiency. "He's been bugging me for the name of my huckleberry supplier." Gavin Vincent was a chef and recent winner of a popular reality TV chef competition show. They'd met in the spring at a weekend retreat gone wrong, and Gavin had stuck around town to open a restaurant with his TV winnings. He'd been delayed opening due to problem after problem but was supposed to soft launch in the next few weeks.

"But after him is Kamari, so I'd recommend being home by six."

"I've never liked having a curfew," Sadie sighed. They'd moved up in line and were almost at the doors.

After a few moments of silence, Kendall broke. "So, are we going to talk about it, or...?"

"I dunno," Sadie said. She looked around. "With people everywhere?"

"But you're doing it, right?"

"Of course, I am," Sadie said. She coughed. Her lungs still hurt.

"Lady Detective Phryne Fisher back at it again," Kendall said, grinning. "Something tells me you'll need your lady's maid, butler, chauffeurs, and wily old aunt to help solve this one."

They stepped through the doors into the warmth of the building's entryway, and the din of outside voices quieted. "I think you're right."

"So, once you vote, your plan is...?"

Sadie thought about it. She needed to know why Paige had disappeared, and when she'd last seen her pen before she could start asking questions. But Paige was still at the police station, it could be a while before she'd be available to talk.

They shuffled down the staircase, the line still moving quickly.

In addition, she should avoid Will, who was absolutely going to expect her to give a statement soon. When her mom had left her, she'd said Arlo had contacted a lawyer and Sadie should expect to hear from them soon.

The planned victory party had been canceled, so Sadie couldn't go there to gather intel. Sadie growled in frustration. "I'm not sure," she said finally. "I'm not sure what to do next."

"I have an idea," Kendall said, patting her good shoulder.

"Great," Sadie said. She felt grateful to have someone else take the lead.

They'd finally reached the front of the line.

The City Clerk, Mrs. Wright, greeted them. Her normally smooth gray bob was a mess around her head, and she had on three pairs of readers: one on her head, one around her neck, and one on her eyes.

"Before you start in on me," she said, "I don't know what they're going to do about the mayoral race, so vote there at your own risk."

Sadie held up her hands. "I wasn't going to ask, but thanks. Been getting that a lot today?"

Mrs. Wright—Sadie didn't actually know her first name, she'd been Mrs. Wright when Sadie was a kid, and she was still Mrs. Wright to her even though Sadie was an adult—sighed heavily. "This wasn't how today was supposed to go."

"Agreed. Now, I was at the fairgrounds this morning..."

"We have another one!" Mrs. Wright called behind her, and an assistant came forward. "Cindy will help you. She'll check the database against your voter ID, and if your ballot wasn't registered, she'll give you a provisional ballot. It has to be provisional in case we recover records from the fairgrounds that have marked ballots."

"Oof," Sadie said, her head starting to hurt. At least she wasn't in charge of those logistics. Cindy helped her quickly, and Sadie marked her ballot without the sentimentality she'd felt earlier. Now, who knew what would happen? If Paige won, would she even serve? If Wade won...she supposed there would either be a special election, or someone would be appointed? Yikes. What a mess.

After her and Kendall had both voted and received their stickers, which they proudly displayed on their coats, they left the building, passing a still-long line of waiting voters.

"This must have been good for turn..." Kendall trailed off as they walked through the doors to the street, the scene outside taking away her words.

"Yikes," Sadie breathed. Parked across the street were multiple news vans. An NBC affiliate from Idaho Falls, over Teton Pass two hours. A CBS affiliate from Bozeman to the north double that. And a few more Sadie didn't recognize—national vans that had moved in from races that weren't quite as exciting as this one had turned out to be?

And their cameras were pointed at them. One dark-haired reporter was giving a live news report, the bright lights illuminating the street behind her in the growing darkness.

With a look at each other, Sadie pulled the hood of her coat up over her head, Kendall doing the same, and then they hurried off in the opposite direction. "This is bad," Sadie said grimly. "All that media in town? That's going to put a lot of pressure on the police."

"Oh, you haven't seen anything, yet" Kendall warned her. "I've got something to show you." She gestured to the SUV idling nearby. "I've got us a lift."

Chapter Six

"Real bummer of a day, sorry about that Sadie," Baxter said from the driver's seat when she slid into the back.

"Thanks, Bax," Sadie said, meeting his eyes in the rearview mirror. He was a huge man of Hawaiian descent, with wavy black hair and a grimace. He'd been a star NFL linebacker until a knee injury had forced him out, and now he did Claire's "heavy work", including driving.

Sully, Claire's assistant, turned around from the passenger seat. He was a tall, thin white man with a crooked nose and nasally voice. He was prone to injuries. Today, he had a bandage over his left eye, which was bruised.

Sadie winced. "Get into another fight with a horse, Sully?"

"I was visiting my niece while Claire was away and she's in a bouncy stage. Took a toddler head direct to the eye."

"Ouch."

"She's a sweet little thing. And deadly," Sully said. "Just like me." He winked at her. "Now, where to?"

Sadie looked at Kendall expectantly.

"Let's do a fairgrounds drive by," she said. They were only a few blocks away.

Sully lifted his eyebrows, but Bax pulled into the street without hesitation.

"Have y'all heard anything about the fire yet? What started it?"

"Well..." Baxter said, turning on to Snow King Avenue. No one said anything.

"Is this part of the show, don't tell gig?" Sadie was getting nervous.

"You'll see," Kendall said.

Her phone buzzed in her pocket, and Sadie pulled it out. A text from Gavin.

> I'm headed to your place in 20 minutes, so if you're not there, let me know where you are instead so I can haul you back to your bed.

> I've got the name of my huckleberry producer for you if you don't tell on me.

The three dots that showed he was typing popped up, but Sadie's attention was pulled from her phone to the scene outside her window.

"Holy..."

"Mmmhmm," Kendall murmured. "I told you, showing would be better."

The fairgrounds exhibit hall fire was out, the roof partially gone, windows busted open with dark smudges of smoke staining them. But that wasn't what had caught her attention.

Parked along the narrow road were more news vans, with big names like CNN on them. And behind the gate, which was barricaded and guarded by two bundled-up Jackson PD officers, was an alphabet soup of law enforcement vehicles.

Sadie read the names, mind boggling. "The ATF is here? And the FBI? What?"

"Federal election interference is a pretty big deal," Sully said. "And bombing a polling place on a federal Election Day apparently counts."

"A bomb?" Sadie gasped. "But I didn't hear...or feel...an explosion?"

"Yeah, you and everyone else," Kendall said, "but that's what Kamari said she heard before they hustled her from the scene. Then Alcohol, Tobacco, and Firearms...which investigates *bombs* came in."

They'd driven past the fairgrounds now.

"Another lap?" Baxter asked.

"One more," Kendall said.

Sadie sat, mouth agape. "So, what you're telling me is...this is going to be really hard."

"There's no flirting information out of Will Nolan, that's for sure," Kendall said. "The town and county aren't even allowed to investigate anymore. They brought in an investigator from the state and they're forming a task force."

"Yikes," Sadie said. But the thought of all that power, all that pressure, being directed at Paige made her feel sick. "But there's no flirting with Will anymore, anyway. He showed up at the hospital all pushy when I was still on pain meds, and I refused to talk to him without a lawyer present."

"That's our girl," Sully said proudly. "You talk to Claire about a lawyer?"

"My dad's on it," she said. "I'll have to give a statement, eventually."

"Maybe you'll be able to give it to a hot FBI agent instead," Kendall mused.

The phone in her lap buzzed again, and Sadie realized she'd been ignoring it, and Gavin had sent a series of texts:

Deal. Immediately.

So, if you're not at your house where are you?

You should let me track your phone like Kendall does.

Seriously now you're freaking me out. I'm going to call your mother.

Sadie tapped back frantically.

We're driving by the fairgrounds. Kendall wanted to give me an idea of the scope of the investigation.

He answered immediately.

You're in my neighborhood, then. Come by. I'll feed y'all dinner.

They drove by the crime scene another time. Her car was still parked in the lot. She wondered when she'd be able to get it back. She checked her watch. It had been less than eight hours since they'd walked into that building so full of confidence. They couldn't have known how things would go.

When they'd passed by again, Sadie tucked her phone away. "Anyone hungry?"

* * *

Gavin had taken over the restaurant formerly known as Carloni's, the classic Italian restaurant Sadie had dined at for every special family occasion when she was a kid. Birthday? Carloni's. Lose a tooth? Carloni's. First period? Carloni's. Awkward teenage date? Carloni's. But the family that had run it for years—surprise, the Carloni's—had grown tired keeping up with the ever-changing Jackson landscape and workforce troubles and had been glad to turn it over to Gavin.

He'd remodeled the space, opening up the low ceiling, removing the wood paneling, and brightening it up with lighter wood on the floors paired with gem tones on the walls. As a brunch and dinner gastropub, Gavin insisted everything had to go from "day-to-night", which Sadie had never really understood, even when it was extolled as a major issue in the fashion magazines of her teens.

It looked great, though. Modern, but classic, and of the place it existed without going full cowboy-mountain-town like so many other establishments in town. Not counting Moose's, of course, which was a historic cabin that had been built onto in the seventies and prided itself on its knotty pine walls and classic Jackson look.

Gavin wrapped her in a hug when she walked in.

"Bad day sis," he said, pulling back to study her, including her splinted arm. "You're pale as a sheet and should be in bed."

"I'm going after this," Sadie promised. She felt it, too. Standing in line in the cold and then seeing the scene at the fairgrounds had taken it out of her.

"Sit, sit," Gavin insisted, showing them to a table. He was a white, dark-haired man with a stubble-covered square jaw, steely gray eyes, and tattoos on both arms. There were rumors he was going to be nominated "sexiest chef" in a nationwide food magazine, and he was dreading it. "I need to do a few things to finish up in the kitchen, but I'll bring it out in a minute."

He disappeared through the swinging door and Sadie, Kendall, Bax, and Sully settled in. There was an extra chair, not including Gavin's.

"Who are we missing?" Sadie asked.

"Me," Claire said, coming in through the front door. "I had to Uber since you took my ride."

"Babe!" Kendall's eyes lit up. "We were supposed to get alone time today, but all this got in the way."

Claire sat next to her, planting a kiss on her cheek. "After this," she promised. She studied Sadie. "Broken wrist, huh?"

"The worst," Sadie sighed. Then she realized what she'd said. "Well. I'm not dead? Or accused of murder? So maybe not the worst?"

"We knew what you meant," Baxter said gently. "It still sucks. They gonna cast it in a few days?"

Spoken like a man who knew his way around injuries. Sadie confirmed it.

"I was scared when I saw you," Claire said. "I was worried you'd hit your head. Why were you still in the building, anyway?"

"When I left my booth, I saw Mateo and Luna, and they couldn't find Paige," Sadie explained. "So, I sent them out the close door and said I'd check the path to the further door."

"That's what firefighters are for," Sully groused. "You could've been more seriously injured. Or killed, too, as an eyewitness."

Sadie thought about that for a minute. "I wasn't a witness, though. I didn't see it happen. I only saw the body."

"The killer might not know that," Sully insisted. "You need to be careful."

Sadie felt nauseous. Maybe she should have stayed in the hospital, even if that meant she didn't get to vote. She would've been safe there, at least.

"I can loan you Bax and Sully," Claire offered.

"What does she need them for?" Gavin asked, his arms laden with dishes he started putting down. He glared at the table. "No one grabbed wine? C'mon."

Baxter jumped up. "I got it." He disappeared behind the bar, then came back with several bottles, brandishing them for Gavin to inspect.

Gavin lifted his brows. "Excellent selections. I love finding your hidden talents."

"He contains multitudes," Sadie said admiringly, and Gavin let out a laugh.

"It's funny you say that, Sadie. Everyone sit."

Everyone settled in, wine was poured, except for Sadie who everyone agreed shouldn't be drinking with the pain meds in her system, and Gavin started passing the family-style dishes around. There was a winter squash salad with blue cheese, pomegranate, and brown sugar vinaigrette, and sliced pork tenderloin glazed in mustard and served with luscious buttery mushrooms. There was warm, house-made sourdough served with sweet butter, green beans tossed in lemon and chili, and enough roasted baby potatoes for everyone to carb load for a marathon.

"How did you make all this so quick?" Kendall said around a mouth of squash.

"Chef magic," Gavin said, shrugging. "I prepped earlier and was going to serve this tomorrow for staff training. I'll make something else in the morning. Now. Why would Sadie need bodyguards?"

Sadie explained the events of the morning. Apparently, Gavin had known she broke her wrist, that Paige's party was canceled, and that Wade was dead, but had no idea the three events were connected. He was notorious for never looking at his phone.

"Well, I'll come stay with you," he offered. It wouldn't be the first time. After they'd met in the spring, Gavin had moved in as a roommate for several months before he got his own housing figured out, something that wasn't easy in a mountain town like Jackson.

"Really?" Sadie asked, her fork hovering over another mushroom.

"Yeah," Gavin said. "I can be intimidating, or so I've heard."

Kendall snorted. "Yeah, you'll do."

"I appreciate it, Gavin. Thank you."

He winked at her. Sadie's heart fluttered a bit, but she tamped it down. Crushing on Gavin was normal for anyone around him, but he liked guys. Unfortunately for her.

"Now, I know we want to talk about Sadie's case," he said. "But I have an announcement. I've decided on a name for the restaurant."

"Oooh!" Claire said, clapping her hands together. "Exciting. Took you long enough, though."

They'd been haranguing him about it for months.

"Well, I got it from Sadie, actually," he said. "And she even said the word tonight."

Sadie thought about it. "Uh..."

"Witness?" Kendall guessed, visibly replaying every word Sadie had said over the course of the evening in her mind.

"Booth?" Sully said, seriously.

"Accused?"

"Murder?"

"You're all terrible at this," Gavin said. "Shush. The name is..."

"Multitudes," Sadie said softly, and Gavin grinned at her.

"That's right. Multitudes." He raised a glass. "To my new baby. May she be popular, efficient, and profitable."

They toasted to that and finished dinner. Sadie checked the time. Almost six, when Kamari was due to take over babysitting duties.

She sent her a quick text.

> Don't tell on me that I'm not there right at six and I'll bring you leftovers from Gavin's restaurant?

> You're testing me, Moose. But my loyalty is to Robin. I'll tell.

Sadie sighed. "I need a ride home so Kamari doesn't call the cavalry."

"I'll box up some leftovers," Gavin said, reading her mind, as usual.

"I'll take you," Kendall offered. "I'll leave my car there and Claire can come pick me up."

Everyone broke to help clean up and get ready to go, leaving Sadie at the table with Claire.

"Where'd you go this morning, Claire?" Sadie asked now that they were alone. "I didn't see you in line behind us?"

"I'm not registered to vote here," Claire admitted. "I came along to help, but I'm still registered in Chicago and voted by mail."

"Oh. Did you see anything suspicious today?"

"Ooh, am I getting the Inspector Moose treatment? I love it." Claire thought about it. "Once you and the Gates-Ortizes went into the voting area, I went back outside. I saw Kamari on my way out, as well as lots of people coming in to vote. I stayed outside near the front to make some phone calls. I had an idea that I might get a good pic of the fam coming out of the polling place. But then the fire alarm went off, and everything went to hell. People came pouring out of the building, and I was looking for everyone. Mateo and Luna came out first, and then we waited for you two."

Sadie frowned. "Wait, I had assumed that Paige was already outside, and that's why Mateo couldn't find her?"

Claire shook her head slowly. "No. It makes me...concerned for her. She was the last one out before you."

Chapter Seven

Sadie made it home with two minutes to spare and two large leftover containers to quell Kamari's need to tattle. Kendall dropped her at the front of the house to spare her mom's watchful eye from the alley, promising to check in the next morning.

Tyrone, her chocolate lab, greeted her at the door, Kamari, righteous, right behind him. She sniffed the leftovers and her shoulders drooped. "I'm starving, so I'm going to skip the being mad at you part of the evening, especially since I can see how tired you are."

"Thanks, friend," Sadie said, moving to the living room and collapsing on one of the couches. Kamari had lit the fire, and it was cozy and warm. Tyrone settled at her feet while Kamari plated her food.

Sadie lifted her phone, checking for messages. She had called and texted Paige multiple times since she'd gotten out of the hospital, to no response. Could she still be at the police station? She had to be. Because otherwise, why would she ignore her? She knew Paige had...a lot on her plate at the moment, but she needed to know how she was doing.

And grill her.

And if Paige wasn't willing to answer her questions, maybe Sadie needed to rethink investigating the case. This was serious business. The FBI and the ATF were involved. Sadie had dealt with annoyance by investigators when she'd poked around, but she couldn't imagine the alphabet agencies would be quite so forgiving.

Kamari interrupted her thoughts by plopping down across from her. She wiggled, trying to get comfortable. "These couches suck," she complained.

"I guess we should go downstairs, then," Sadie said pointedly. She still wasn't over the one-two punch of Kendall and Kamari, often collectively called KitKat, convincing her it was time to sell her beloved beaten up leather sofas in the community yard sale in the spring, only to have the two of them snatch them up for their own houses.

"Mmm," Kamari groaned after her first bite. "Gavin's an angel."

"He is," Sadie agreed. "When you've filled your tummy enough to talk, tell me about your day and I'll tell you about mine?"

Kamari shoved another bite of food in. "You start," she said, mouth full.

With a deep breath, Sadie started at the beginning. When she'd caught up to present time, Kamari had slowed down. She took a gulp of the wine she'd brought with her, then reached into her jacket pocket and tossed a bottle of pills to Sadie, followed by a gentler nudge of a bottle of water. "You're due for a pain pill," she said. "Now settle in for a story."

Sadie took the pill gratefully.

"It was a busy morning at the polling place. There were lots of familiar faces. I got there at six, the polls opened at seven. We didn't have any problems until Wade showed up and started glad-handing in the line. I gave him a warning, and then the head election judge gave him a formal warning when he didn't stop."

"Who was he there with?"

Kamari squinted at her. "His wife and his campaign manager. I lost track of him, not sure where he went."

"His mother wasn't there?"

"I don't know what his mother looks like, but I didn't see any older women hanging around him."

"Did his wife seem...happy?"

Kamari frowned. "I don't know, Moose. I was watching them closely, but not that closely. She seemed like any other rich dude's wife to me. Can I continue?"

Sadie urged her on.

"Y'all came in and held up my line—"

"Sorry."

Kamari waved her off, setting her empty plate aside. "From the time you entered until I saw smoke and pulled the fire alarm was about fifteen minutes."

Sadie gaped at her. "You pulled the alarm? So, you saw the whole thing! How did the fire start?"

"I didn't see it start. I saw smoke coming from the supply closet, so I pulled the alarm. There wasn't flame at first, or heat, but by the time I made sure the main room was evacuating, there was heat and flame was licking out underneath the door."

"Kamari! That's so scary. And you're a hero!"

She shrugged it off. "Literally my job today," she said nonchalantly. "Anyway, after I made sure the other room was evacuating and those election judges were doing their jobs, I evacuated out the front door and called 911 for the fire department which was already on its way."

"And then?"

"There's not much to report, which is what I already told the police when I gave my statement."

"Without a lawyer?" Sadie cringed.

"I FaceTimed my cousin," Kamari said. "It wasn't official, but it got me through it without a hassle."

"I can't decide if that was smart or not. You were the only one in the vestibule besides voters, right? What if they decide you put the ignition device or whatever it was in there?"

"Oh, they might decide that," Kamari sighed. "But I didn't do it. I don't know, Moose, I just wanted to do the right thing and get them the info right away."

"Which is directly opposite of what I did," Sadie groaned. "I basically told Will to fuck off."

"He deserved it. I would've told him the same if I was there. Questioning someone under duress and the influence of pain meds. How dare he."

"So, you gave your statement and were free to go?"

"Yep. Took the longest shower of my life, then volunteered at a different polling place."

"I appreciate your commitment to civics."

"This shit is real to me, Moose."

"Me, too, Kamari," Sadie promised. And Sadie meant it. "So, you didn't see anybody or anything suspicious at all?"

"This is Jackson Hole. I saw tons of suspicious folks. White dudes with dreadlocks. Women with handbags that cost more than my car. So, so many Canada Goose jackets. But no, I didn't see anybody near the supply closet all morning. Plus, it was locked. I couldn't get in, either."

"Could the fire have been an accident then? But then why is ATF here?"

"Yeah, I'm supposed to be expecting a visit from an ATF agent since I was the first one to see the smoke. I hope he's hot."

"I hope so, too, for your sake," Sadie said absently. None of this made sense. Were they dealing with two crimes? Someone set a fire, and someone murdered Wade? Or one crime—the fire was started by the same person that killed Wade? Or another possibility. The fire was an accident, and someone murdered Wade? Sadie knew, at the least, that someone had murdered him. She'd seen the pen up close. That made her think of something else.

"Did you see everyone come out of the building?"

"I was at the front, so I didn't see anyone come out the side doors. I looked for y'all, though, and eventually saw Mateo with Luna. And Claire was already outside when I came out. Loitering. Which is not allowed on Election Day." She took a deep breath and reached for Sadie's unsplinted hand. "I was so worried about you."

"Thanks, friend. I was okay. Just...stumbling over a dead body."

"Again."

"Yes. Again."

"Well, how are you going to solve this one?"

Sadie considered it. "I need to talk to Paige. I don't understand why she didn't leave with her family. I know she didn't kill him. But it looks bad. And besides that...I suppose I need to talk to Wade's wife and campaign manager since they were both there. And hope I can glean information about the fire from a federal investigation. I'll need to be really, really lucky."

Kamari stood. "If anyone can do it, it's you, Moose. Paige will need you now. With that weird rumor going around this morning, plus this and the uncertainty of the race..."

"The race!" Sadie grabbed her phone. "The results should be posted, it's after seven!"

"I wouldn't count on it," Kamari said on her way to the kitchen. "It's going to take a while with all this chaos."

* * *

Kamari was right, the results weren't posted yet. A notice on the website said that because of unforeseen circumstances—which was a delicate way to put it—results would be significantly delayed, and preliminary counts weren't expected until the next morning at the earliest.

"Well boo," Sadie sighed.

"Boo what, dear?" Penny said, sweeping into the room. She paused for effect, and Sadie took in her outfit with reluctant amusement. She wore a tight, navy blue, mermaid skirt that showed off her generous curves and a keyhole white button-up that showed her cleavage. A vintage 'Votes for Women' pin was pinned on her shirt. A short-brimmed straw hat over her hair, currently dyed coal black in a rejection of her long-running Barbie pink era, completed the look.

"I don't know that the suffragette's skirts were *quite* that tight," Sadie said dryly.

"But you recognized my homage! These national piranhas all pretended they didn't," she pouted. "Sorry I'm late, by the way." She giggled. "I haven't babysat in a while." She stopped halfway into the room. "Wait, do I smell Gavin food?"

"In the kitchen," Sadie said. "Go on and load up if Kamari didn't eat everything. Then come back. I want to know every-thing you know."

"Ooooooh, and do I know stuff," Penny called, already in the kitchen.

Kamari came back to take Tyrone out for a walk, and soon Penny settled in on the couch across from her, shoving food into her mouth. Sadie checked her phone again. No calls or messages from Paige. Or Mateo.

She sent another one, getting desperate.

Worried about you! Please check in!

"Trying to get a hold of Paige?" Penny asked, her voice sympathetic. "It's not gonna work. She's still at the police station."

"What?" Sadie was shocked.

"Oh yeah, she's at the top of the list. It's serious."

Sadie wouldn't have dreamed, ever, that Paige would still be there. Poor Luna, without her mama! Sadie was overcome, tears prickling at her eyes.

Penny groaned when she noticed, putting down her plate and coming around the coffee table to sit next to her, pulling her into a hug. "I'm sorry, babe. I didn't mean to be flippant. I'm worried about her, too."

"I know she didn't do this," Sadie said, her voice quavering. "I just know it. We must figure this out. For her. For Luna!"

"We will. So, take a deep breath, wipe your eyes, and buck the fuck up," Penny said sternly. "I need to eat, and then I'll tell you everything, as long as you do the same."

So, Sadie started again. How many times had she told the story today? The altercation in the morning. The weird insinuation about Paige. The damage control they'd attempted. Going to the polling place. Running into Wade. Going into the voting booth. Smelling smoke and hearing the alarm. And then the rest. Looking for Paige, finding a dead body, breaking her wrist, waking up in the hospital.

"Oof," Penny said when she was done. "That deserves ice cream. I'll be back."

Sadie let her head droop onto the back of the couch while she waited for her to return. The day was catching up to her. And man, her arm really hurt. Hadn't she just taken a pill? She woke up when a bowl of ice cream was plopped in her lap.

"Eat," Penny said. "It will keep you awake while I tell you my side."

Penny heard the initial call for a fire at the polling place over the scanner and called Randall to tell him. She sped over there to take photos, which had become the pictures national media was using. She tried not to preen at that part. She'd been pretty wrapped up in the drama of it and arrived in time to see an ambulance speeding away, not knowing that Sadie was inside of it.

Once the police were established, they pushed the media—just Randall and Penny at that point—out of the gate, so they watched them put the fire out through the chain link. Everyone who hadn't left the scene was herded into another building to stay warm before their statements were taken. Everyone except Madison Fisher, who refused to move. She stood outside, crying and begging for information.

"A pitiful sight," Penny clucked.

And then the coroner arrived. And Madison fell onto her knees, screaming.

"Oof," Sadie said, the flavor of praline pecan on her tongue. "That's rough. Poor Madison."

"She left soon after, shuttled away by someone Randall identified as a family friend."

"Huh."

"Anyway, after that not a lot happened. There were a lot of cops."

"Including *your* cop?" Sadie asked. Penny had been dating Officer Greg Knott of the Jackson Police Department for almost a year.

Penny pouted. "Greg's in Wisconsin for a family thing."

"Ooh, that's bad news for us."

"Very." Penny dropped her spoon into her bowl with a clank. "Plus, I'm mad he didn't ask me to be a plus one."

Sadie winced. There was nothing Penny loved more than being a plus one.

"A wedding?"

"A funeral," Penny said morosely.

"Even worse." Penny loved a good funeral. Sadie tried to suppress a yawn. It wasn't even eight o'clock. Gavin wasn't here yet for his overnight shift. And who was supposed to come at eight? There'd been a schedule until ten according to Kendall.

"I can tell you're at the end of your rope," Penny said with sympathy. "I'll be quick with the rest. So, after the coroner arrived, the Wyoming Department of Criminal Investigation arrived."

"How'd they get there so fast?" If the DCI investigator was based in Cheyenne, the capital of Wyoming, it was an eight-hour drive to Jackson.

"I'm guessing a plane," Penny shrugged. "Anyway, they arrived, and then a crime scene investigation unit, and then they just kept on coming. The state fire marshall. The ATF. The FBI. More I didn't even recognize. The ATF coming was our first indication it could've been a bomb that started the fire."

"But there wasn't an explosion or anything," Sadie protested.

"Smoke bomb?" Penny suggested. "I was googling it."

Sadie yawned again, unable to suppress it this time.

"Okay, okay, fast forward...They released a statement about an active crime scene and released that Wade was deceased around noon. I'm sure they would've rather waited, but it was obvious at that point he was missing in action on Election Day. Then they held a press conference this afternoon when the national press started arriving, but they had nothing new to report. Active investigation. Election implications. Forming a task force."

Sadie sighed. "So, we've got...about nothing to go on."

"A little more than that, but I agree, we've got to talk to Paige."

"Tomorrow," Sadie vowed. "But I won't ever make it if I don't go to bed. Tell whoever comes to relieve you thanks for me, and Gavin knows where his bed is."

She stayed up long enough to set phone alarms to take her pain medication throughout the night, then settled into her pillows, arm propped up. She dropped off to the sound of Kamari and Tyrone coming back inside and low voices talking in the living room.

Maybe when she woke up, the whole day would be a dream, instead of the nightmare it'd become.

Chapter Eight

Normally, Sadie awoke at four in the morning on Wednesdays to go to work, the one morning she opened instead of Sage or Max Ridgely, her two assistant bakers. But her dad had already claimed the shift the day before, so Sadie slept until her next pain pill was due at eight. After she took it, she tried to sleep more, but it was useless. She was up.

She sprawled on the bed, scrolling her phone. Her heart skipped when she saw a text from Paige. It had come through at three in the morning.

> Finally home. Awful day. Am okay. Will call tomorrow when I wake up. Hope your arm is okay.

It wasn't, but it would be. But would Paige? She'd been working for so long for this step in her political career. And now...even if she won the race, was it a race well won if her rival was dead?

Sadie checked the news. It was a special kind of surreal to see a familiar cable news reporter doing a live report in front of the famed antler arches in the middle of town. When was the last time her town had garnered this kind of attention? She grimaced at the salacious headlines. They'd found a picture of Paige in a pink vagina hat at a pro-choice rally in the town square a couple years ago and were using that instead of her official town council picture. Sadie studied it. She looked good. Bright, fiery, and determined. Even if pink clashed with her strawberry blonde hair. But using it would surely ignite conservative media.

Sure enough.

LIBERAL MAYORAL CANDIDATE CONNECTED TO RIVAL DEVELOPER'S DEATH one headline read. SMALL TOWN SHOCKER: FIRE, DEATH, AND SMALL-TOWN POLITICS read one think piece's moniker. A think piece. Seemed a little early for that. Sadie noted the task force had scheduled a press conference at noon. That was good. Gave her something to plan her day around.

She flipped over to a social media app, scrolling through the town gossip group. She'd found hot tips there before, though they were usually for excellent garage sales, not murders.

Instead, she found the town was going through an existential crisis. Someone had posted the town charter, and the same people that had claimed to be infectious disease experts during the pandemic were now acting as constitutional law fellows, claiming any number of things about the state of the town if a mayor wasn't elected.

There was an entire thread talking about how Paige could have done it. Sadie couldn't believe the theories being floated about her gentle friend, the meditation coach and therapist who relocated spiders instead of smashing them. Goodness.

There was a post memorializing Wade, and Sadie scrolled through that one quickly. Who had his friends been? She really didn't know much about him now that she thought about it.

She'd need to carve out time to learn more about his past, about his present in Jackson.

She closed the group, already exhausted by the rhetoric and all-caps posts.

There was a gentle knock at her door and Sadie called for whoever it was to come in. It was her mom.

"Hey babe." Robin set a steaming cup of tea on Sadie's nightstand. Tyrone pushed past her, nosing Sadie with concern. She patted his head and leaned over to kiss his furry brown nose.

"Morning, mom."

"How were your adventures yesterday?"

Sadie blanched. "Who told?"

"I have eyes everywhere," Robin said.

Some things never changed, Sadie supposed.

"I presume you have more investigating to do today?" she asked.

"I've gotta figure this out, mom."

"You do," Robin agreed. "So, I made you breakfast. It's ready when you are."

Sadie relaxed. She'd expected her mom to fight her, especially since the doctor had told her yesterday she needed to take it easy until she could get a cast on. Traipsing around Jackson investigating a bombing and murder wasn't following those directions, exactly. But Robin loved Paige, too.

"Gavin had to run, something about a band of miscreants eating all his food last night so he had to do an early prep. He wanted to report a quiet night, complain about the comfort of his assigned bed, and suggest we switch Tyrone's food, so he'll stop farting so much."

Tyrone's ears perked at his name, and Sadie patted his head. "Oh, Ty, did you stink up poor Gavin's room last night?" He panted, grinning. "Good boy."

"He said he'd be back tonight. You're so blessed with good friends. And handsome ones."

That was true.

"So, what's your plan for the day?"

Sadie thought about it. "It's tricky. I might drop by the bakery this morning to catch up on gossip. Then I need to talk to Paige and figure out a few things about yesterday. Might try to sneak into a press conference with Penny at noon. And then, who knows?"

"Add in a meeting with your new lawyer at one, please. They'll meet you here. I'm not sure when they'll schedule your statement, but I won't complain or tell your doctor if you promise to nap after that meeting."

"Deal."

Mother satisfied and legal requirements in motion, Sadie cleaned herself up and ate breakfast. Dressing for the cold with her arm in a splint and brace was a challenge. With her mom's help, she dressed in a soft Moose's Bakery t-shirt with the sling over the top and a sweater draped over the arm. Her coat was the same situation. She slipped her pain pills into her pocket, kissed her mom, patted Tyrone on the head, and set out.

It was a cold, crisp day. While they hadn't seen snow on the valley floor this fall yet, the mountains were covered in it. Sadie hadn't checked the forecast, but she wouldn't be surprised if they woke up to snow sometime this week. It was time. The seemingly endless Jackson Hole winter was beginning, the always-too-short autumn ending.

The walk from her house to the bakery was only three blocks, ones she knew well. She'd walked them her entire life. Her parents had started the bakery together in the early years of their marriage, and Sadie had grown up there. When Sadie took over the business, she also purchased the home she'd grown up in so they could retire to Arizona. Sometimes Sadie wondered what would have happened had she decided *not* to take over the family business after she came home after college, but her musings never got her far. She couldn't imagine a different life. She loved her bakery, her friends, and her town.

A block away from Moose's, a voice called her name, and she looked up from the sidewalk. She froze. It was Nancy Fisher.

* * *

Sadie had thought the woman was short yesterday, but today she seemed to have curled into herself. She wasn't just small, she was frail. Her eyes were red, the bags underneath indicative of a sleepless night. The poor woman had lost her son. And while Sadie hadn't liked the man much, and Nancy had left a real sour taste in her mouth yesterday, her heart went out to her. She couldn't imagine the loss she was feeling.

Sadie slowly approached her. She stood in the middle of the sidewalk, shoulders drooping.

"Mrs. Fisher," Sadie said softly. "I'm so sorry for your loss."

Nancy sniffled and nodded. "Thank you," she said graciously. She took a deep breath. "I was looking for you. I wanted to...apologize for yesterday. We were all so keyed up about the election, and now...none of it seems to matter anymore."

Sadie swallowed hard. "No apologies are needed." Though she would pass it on to Kendall, who was still baffled at how her good deed had been turned around on her so fast. "But I accept it, nonetheless. Now, can we get you out of the cold? Can I get you a cup of coffee and something to eat at the bakery?" Sadie gestured down the block, where she could just see the log cabin roofline of the bakery between its florist and bookstore neighbors.

"No," Nancy shook her head. "I don't have an appetite. I'm headed—" she took a deep, shuddering breath, tears springing to her eyes. "To the funeral home now to meet poor Madison. She's devastated. But I also..." she scrubbed her forearm over her eyes, dashing away the tears. She reached into the large purse she carried over her arm. Sadie stiffened. What was she pulling out? The woman's apology seemed genuine. But she'd seen how unhinged she could be yesterday.

Bracing herself to run, Sadie watched her hand closely. But Nancy pulled out a large envelope, not a gun. Phew.

Nancy held it out. Sadie stared at it.

"Take it," she said. "I told you I had information about Paige. I was going to release it yesterday. And then everything fell apart." Her voice wavered again. "But I think it's important for you to see this."

Dread pooled in her stomach. She didn't want to know anything else that made her best friend look more like a murderer. But this was the responsibility she'd assigned to herself, wasn't it? If she was going to solve the case, she had to evaluate all the information, and this weird rumor Nancy had alluded to yesterday...well, Nancy Fisher had receipts, apparently. Sadie took the envelope reluctantly, pulling off her glove so she could open it one handed.

"Did you hurt yourself?" Nancy asked, suddenly noticing her arm in the sling.

Tripping over your son's dead body.

"Fell yesterday," Sadie said, trying to keep her voice light. "Cracked my wrist. I'll be okay though, no surgery needed."

Nancy murmured something, but Sadie didn't hear her. She was too busy looking at the photos that spilled out of the envelope. They'd been taken from a distance but were perfect quality. Had Nancy hired a private detective to take these? That was so extreme.

But what she'd caught was...damning.

She wasn't sure exactly what they meant, but Nancy Fisher had been right. She'd found something that made her call her entire friendship with Paige into question. The one thing she'd always thought would be impossible.

But here it was, the evidence.

Of a secret meeting between Paige...and Merritt West and his gorgeous fiancé.

Chapter Nine

Sadie flipped through the pictures as well as she could one handed. Her mouth was dry. Why would her best friend meet with Merritt and not tell her?

"What...what are these?" Sadie finally asked. She tried to keep her face neutral. Nancy didn't need to know that these affected her. Because why would Paige meeting with Merritt be politically damning? All she saw here was a betrayal of their friendship.

Nancy drew her shoulders back a little, becoming more the defiant woman she was yesterday. "That's your friend meeting with the head of Gotham Enterprises, Nora Mooney. I don't know who the man is."

Sadie swallowed hard. That name rang a bell. Gotham Enterprises? Why did that sound familiar?

"I don't get it," Sadie said, cycling through the pictures once more before sliding them back in the envelope. She tucked it carefully under her slinged arm. Might as well make it work.

Nancy let out an impatient noise. "Remember the whole free money thing? Everyone thought it was my son being shady, but it turned out to be this philanthropic organization, Gotham Enterprises, remember?"

"Oh. Oh!" The pieces were falling into place. This spring, during the annual charity tag sale in town square, the one she'd sold her beloved couches in, a booth had given away hundred-dollar bills. They'd given away tens of thousands of dollars, and there had been a lot of speculation over who was behind it. Finally, the organization had come forward in an ad in the *Journal*, stating that they were a non-partisan philanthropic organization and had not worked with any candidate. But that hadn't been Sadie's first run in with them.

Around Valentine's Day, Sadie had supposedly won a new reality TV show called Random Acts of Kindness. She'd been challenged to bake an extraordinary number of cookies to give away at the local schools with a tight deadline and had completed the work with a lot of extra help and overtime paid. She'd then been surprised with TV cameras and her prize for completing the challenge: two brand new delivery vans already emblazoned with the Moose's logo. It had all seemed incredibly fishy, but her lawyers couldn't find anything wrong with the presented documentation, so she'd accepted the prize. And the organization that had ordered the cookies in the first place? Gotham Enterprises.

"You see?" Nancy Fisher said impatiently. "Paige was working with them. All that so-called philanthropy to prop up her campaign!"

"But...without publicly connecting to Paige, how did their efforts benefit her?" Sadie asked slowly, trying to figure out the logic.

Nancy shook her head sourly. "Paying off school lunch debt? Direct payments to anyone that asked for them? Donating to public housing projects? Those sound like the liberal ideas your friend supports."

Sadie bit off a rude reply. Those sounded like *humane* things to her, not political ideas. The woman was grieving. She needed to be nice. Even if this information was...too much for her to handle at the moment. She needed a few minutes to think. To figure out exactly what this meant. Why was Merritt's fiancé the head of Gotham Enterprises? Why had Gotham Enterprises messed with her life? The reality TV show had never aired and any traces of it had been scrubbed from the Internet. And Gavin, who had won that giant reality TV prize, had told her it was totally unheard of to take possession of a prize before the show aired.

Sadie shook her head, trying to clear it. She wasn't going to figure this out standing on the sidewalk. And her arm was starting to hurt. She needed to prop it up on something.

"Well," Sadie said, worrying her lip. "I appreciate you giving me this information. I'll look into it."

"You do that," Nancy said. "I'll be releasing it! I've already told the investigators about it. Everyone will know what Paige did soon enough." Her voice was dripping with vitriol, and Sadie felt her back go up.

"This looks weird, but I still believe in my friend," Sadie said. And she did. She didn't understand, but she believed in her. Paige would have an explanation. She knew it.

"She's a murderer," Nancy said, teeth gritting together. "She murdered my son!"

Sadie took a step back. "Respectfully, she didn't. Now, I'm wishing you well. Be gentle with yourself."

Nancy scoffed. "I should've known you wouldn't see the truth. Give me those photos back!"

Sadie frowned. "No."

Nancy stepped forward. "Give them to me!" Her voice was raised. Sadie looked around. It would not be good to draw a crowd right now.

Then she heard a camera shutter, rapidly, from a few feet away. It was too late. They were already making a scene. Sadie turned to find the noise, seeing a photographer there. The town was crawling with media. Had they been following Nancy, or were they just out trolling for drama?

"You're causing a scene," Sadie said through gritted teeth. "If you want them back, you can get them once I've made copies."

Nancy glanced at the camera, some of the fight leaving her. "I have my own copies," she groused. "It's fine. I have to go. Stay away from me!" She stomped off, and Sadie took a deep breath. What a grouchy old woman.

She turned resolutely away from the photographer and started walking again, getting as far away from them as she could.

* * *

When she reached the front door of the bakery, she was out of breath. She couldn't tell if the photographer had followed her. She ducked into the bakery and peered out the window, thankful for the first time that there wasn't a line out the door. She didn't see anyone following her.

"Woah there, Sadie," Max said from behind her, a bus bin in their hands. "You okay?"

Sadie looked up and down the street again, then relaxed. "Yeah, I think so." She turned. "How are things here?" The bakery was quiet, half the tables open amidst the mid-morning lull before lunch.

"We were slammed this morning. All those news crews needed boxes and boxes of pastries. But we were prepared. Your Dad's been telling us tales about the media presence during the Yellowstone fires of '88 and apparently this doesn't compare."

Sadie bit back a smile. She'd heard all her dad's stories. She was thankful he was there to tell them to rally the bakery while she was out of commission.

Max watched her thoughtfully. They were nonbinary and used they/them pronouns. In their mid-twenties, Max was tall and slim with baker's arms and short black hair. They were Northern Arapahoe and had grown up on the Wind River Reservation. They'd been at the bakery about a year, and Sadie wasn't sure how she'd survived without them.

Max swayed closer to speak quietly. "The table of regulars has been waiting around for you, though. You should've come in the back." And that's when Sadie realized what that itchy feeling between her shoulder blades was. It wasn't someone watching her from outside. It was that she was being watched from *inside*. Great.

Sadie glanced behind her and Opal Fowler, the group leader, waved. She slid the manila envelope out from under her arm and handed it to Max. "Hold on to this for me?" Max nodded their assent. She wouldn't be getting out of this, bad arm or no. "If I'm not released from their grip in ten minutes, please invent a crisis for me," Sadie whispered to Max, who laughed. That wasn't very promising.

Sadie slunk over to the table and sat in the chair Opal offered. The hot seat. She scanned the faces of the other women. There were seven of them total, all older women retired from their day jobs. They came to the bakery every morning, took up the best corner table, and solved all the town's problems by the time they left around ten—or at least they did in their own heads. They were still here, though, which meant they had business with her. Sadie shouldn't be surprised, she supposed. She could only hope they had information *for her* and weren't just going to grill her. Her eyes caught Gretchen Whitehouse's, and she started, remembering for the first time that Gretchen had been at the polling place yesterday, too. She opened her mouth to ask her about it but was interrupted.

"How's your arm?" Opal asked, a note of concern in her voice. Opal was a white woman in her seventies, barely five feet tall, with a penchant for Gucci tracksuits and oversized gold sunglasses she wore inside because of her cataracts. She usually carried her teacup poodle, Prada, with her everywhere, smuggling him into the bakery in her fancy handbag, but Sadie didn't see her purse today. Maybe Prada was at home.

"It's broken," Sadie sighed. "I have to go back tomorrow for them to check it when the swelling has gone down, and hopefully they'll be able to cast it."

"Oh, you poor dear," clucked Denise Garza, a Hispanic woman with long hair just turning silver. She'd put down her knitting to study Sadie. "It's been a rough twenty-four hours for you."

"Rough year," Zoey Fremont, a white woman who always wore her hair in two gray French braids, corrected. Her sister, Chloe, the kinder of the two, jabbed her with an elbow. "What?" Zoey complained, rubbing her side. "It's true."

"It might be true," Chloe said softly, reaching over to pat Sadie's hand. She had a sleek gray bob and wore large, thick glasses that magnified her eyes. "But that doesn't mean we need to rub it in. We're here for you, Sadie. And for Paige."

"We always have been," Lilith Dormer, a white woman in her sixties, said. She was a widow with a sharp widow's peak and an abundance of clacking bracelets. "Remember when you, Paige, and Merritt broke one of my windows playing ball when you were kids? I didn't even make you pay for it."

Sadie frowned. That wasn't *exactly* how she remembered that incident—and she didn't like the reminder of Merritt when those pictures were still burning a hole in her brain— but it was true. The table of regulars had been her parents' table of regulars before they were hers, though some of the faces had changed. This group had been the first to buy tickets to her high school drama performances, the first to support whatever school fundraising project she was working on, the first to order her more adventurous new bakes. And they were steadfast supporters of the bakery, even if they drove Sadie bananas.

"You're all kind," Sadie said. "My arm hurts, but I'll be okay. I'm most worried for Paige."

"Bad news," Millie Yin intoned, her eyes closed. Millie was Chinese, round like a pear, and had been old since Sadie was a child. She spent most of her time in the bakery napping, or pretending to.

Sadie met Gretchen's eyes. "It was a hard day for you, too, Gretch," Sadie said. "Can you tell me what you saw at the polling place?"

Gretchen sniffed. Her paperback was already tucked into her tote bag, her hands clasped in front of her. She was prepared to tell her story. "Well," she said, taking a sip of her herbal tea, "I was checking in a voter when I heard the fire alarm go off. I only smelled smoke then. We'd practiced an evacuation before, of course, but we never imagined we'd have to go through with it."

"Did it go the way you practiced?" Sadie asked.

"Not at all," Gretchen sighed. "People ran every which way, no orderly lines moving toward the exits. I was worried I'd be trampled! Plus, the other election judges abandoned the poll books, so I had to grab all of them."

"That was brave of you," Sadie said gently, "but people are more important than poll books. I'm glad you got out safely. Which door did you exit?"

"I went out the door on the north side of the building," Gretchen said, thinking about it. "The opposite of you? I didn't see you come out."

"Yeah," Sadie said. "I went out the south door after Mateo couldn't find Paige."

There was an awkward silence at the table.

"Well, that's the thing we wanted to tell you," Opal said gently. She nodded at Gretchen. "Gretchen, go ahead."

Gretchen sighed and put her shoulders back, looking directly at Sadie. "As I was leaving, I turned to check the room. And saw Paige and Wade arguing."

Chapter Ten

Sadie barely remembered wrapping up the conversation with the table of regulars and stumbling into her office, Gretchen's words still running through her head. She sank into her chair and stared at the ceiling. They'd been arguing. They'd been *seen* arguing! Gretchen had absolutely said that in her statement. No wonder they had kept Paige at the police station until three in the morning, even with a lawyer present. With the evidence piling up against Paige, Sadie was surprised she hadn't been charged. Were they just waiting for forensics to come back?

Or was she looking at this all wrong?

Sadie remembered when she'd been accused of killing her lifelong nemesis, Sloan Brackenridge, last fall. More than one of her close friends—heck, even her own mother—had asked her, seriously, if she'd done it. But Paige never had, not once. She wondered now if Paige had ever had doubts like Sadie was having.

But the evidence—Wade's mother's pictures, that he'd been killed with Paige's pen, that they'd been seen arguing, that Paige hadn't been where she should be at the time of the murder—it didn't add up for Sadie. What would Paige's motive be? She had known that it was Wade's mother who said she had info on her, so killing Wade wouldn't remove the threat. And she didn't need to kill him to win the election—surely, she was going to win, anyway!

Which made Sadie realize, it was past time early returns were in.

She woke up her computer with a jiggle of the mouse and navigated to a browser window, then googled 'Jackson WY mayor results'.

The page brought up more salacious headlines, but the top one answered her question.

TOP SUSPECT MAYORAL CANDIDATE IN LEAD OVER MURDERED RIVAL

Goodness. Headline writers were working overtime on this one. She scrolled down until she found the county website, then clicked the link. With seventy-five percent of the vote in, Paige was leading Wade by 1,000 votes. It would be practically impossible for Wade to close that gap, but with a lot of the late counts coming in from the emergency poll site, who knew. Maybe once people knew he was dead, they voted for him instead. Some sort of sympathy vote?

There was a knock on her office door, and then Kendall poked her head in. She held the manila envelope she'd given to Max. "Woah, Boss. What are these? Wild!"

Sadie sighed. "You looked?"

"Of course I looked. We all looked. What are we going to do about it?"

"Let me ask you a question. What do you think they mean?"

Kendall came inside, shutting the door behind her and leaning on it. She tapped the envelope on her thigh absently. She was always moving, eternally full of energy. "Without context, it looks like Paige might have been taking money from Merritt for the campaign?"

Sadie blanched. "Ugh, yeah. I could see that. Without context. But Paige wouldn't do that! I've seen her records, they're all legitimate. And we didn't have any expenses I can't explain."

"But it might be enough to muddy the waters," Kendall said. "More than that, though, I'm concerned that she's hanging with Merritt without talking to you about it."

"Yeah," Sadie said, swallowing hard. "I haven't quite gotten over that, either. But back to context. I got those from Nancy Fisher. And she said that the woman in the photos is the—wait for it—head of Gotham Enterprises."

Kendall's eyes got wide. She mimicked the head blown gesture. "Gotham Enterprises? Like the cookie and van people? And the free money? What? That's..." her eyes snapped to Sadie's. "Wait. Remember when you found out Merritt was a secret almost-billionaire?"

Sadie rolled her eyes. "How could I forget?" That'd been near the end of their whirlwind romance. Merritt worked for the State Department in a secretive diplomatic position, but in college he'd patented a device and sold it to a defense contractor for a significant sum, which he'd invested. He'd promised he wasn't a billionaire...but was maybe close. Sadie's least favorite thing.

"And instead of being our 007, what did you call him?"

Sadie blinked. She'd always teased Merritt that his discrete life was evidence he was a secret agent. But when she'd found out about the money, she'd called him—

"Batman!" She shouted it, standing up suddenly.

Kendall was jumping up and down. "Yes! Batman! Gotham! It was him, this whole time!" Kendall threw her arms around her, squeezing her.

Sadie hissed, pulling away her bad arm. "Sorry, sorry," Kendall said. "I'm just excited to figure out the puzzle. I never get to figure out the puzzle!"

Sadie sank back into her chair. There wasn't really enough room in her office for both of them to stand. "But why? Why would he do all those things?"

Kendall grinned. "Love."

"He's engaged to someone else!"

"So, he's a bit of a fixer upper," she shrugged.

Sadie rolled her eyes. "Too much of a fixer upper for me. But you've uncovered something important, Kendall. I can't believe this."

"You have to talk to him."

Sadie shook her head vigorously. "If he wanted to talk to me, he could. He knows where I work, he knows where I live, he knows my email address."

"You blocked him on social media, though..."

Sadie cringed. She had done that. After he'd been spotted with the blonde with the big rock, she'd cut off their digital connection, where she was the only follower on his secret Instagram account.

"It's so romantic," Kendall sighed. "You told him you hated billionaires, he confessed he had a bunch of money, so then he gave away a lot of it—to you and causes you love—to show you his feelings."

"That is an unproven hypothesis," Sadie said, her heart pounding fast. "And one disproved by the existence of his fiancé." But she felt something coming alive inside her, something she hadn't felt in a while. Hope. Hope that maybe they could have a future together.

There was a knock at the door. "What's all the racket in here?" Arlo asked, poking his head in.

"Merritt's secretly in love with Sadie and spending a bunch of money on the town to show her," Kendall said breathlessly.

Arlo didn't even blink. "That boy's never been good at talking about his feelings. Listen, this came for you."

He held out a blank card-sized envelope.

Great. Another piece of mysterious mail. Sadie eyed it warily. "Who brought it?"

"I dunno," Arlo said, puzzled. "It was left on a table in the dining room, but it has your name on it. Max found it when they were bussing." He waved it at her. "It won't bite, girl. Take it."

Sadie did so, reluctantly, and Arlo left. He left almost too easily. He was a curious guy and wasn't someone to walk away from a mystery. Sadie groaned inwardly. No wonder she was the way she was. But she'd deal with whatever her dad was up to later.

"Want me to open it?" Kendall asked.

Sadie handed it to her. "Sure."

Kendall carefully ripped the envelope open. Inside was a single piece of paper, folded. Kendall skimmed it, then frowned, turning it around so Sadie could see it.

Sadie,

I can't come see you. I'm being watched. I'm sure you have a lot of questions. I want you to stay out of all this. I didn't do it, and I'll be vindicated, eventually. Love you.

Paige

P.S. Mom is dropping this off while she picks up pastries for us.

P.P.S. I'm okay.

"Shit," Sadie said. "I need to talk to her. There are too many questions only she can answer."

"And she has her hands full," Kendall said. "There's an entire graduating class of law enforcement officers breathing down her neck. She's trying to protect you."

Of course she was.

That's who she was.

Who she'd always been.

And Sadie believed her. She hadn't murdered Wade. The doubts she'd had earlier...they were gone now. And she wouldn't let her friend take the fall. She would find out who did it. Even if that meant talking to the one person she promised she wouldn't ever talk to again.

* * *

Penny thought the idea of Sadie crashing the press conference was brilliant.

Probably too brilliant.

Sadie flat out refused to wear a disguise, but when Penny picked her up outside the bakery—her own car still being at the fairgrounds and Sadie not being too keen on making herself noticed by asking when she could get it—there was a bag in the seat full of options, anyway.

"Do you just...carry this around?" Sadie asked, pawing through the carefully packaged wigs, glasses, and hats in the bag.

"Of course," Penny said. "I live a life of high drama and intrigue, you know."

"As the office manager at the local paper."

Penny sniffed. "I've been promoted to general manager."

"What? Congrats!"

Penny grinned. "I tricked Randall into signing the paper

after he'd had one too many at happy hour. He's not pleased, but he's too proud to admit I got one over on him."

"You terrify me, Penny."

"Greg has taken to calling me his little manic pixie nightmare," she said cheerfully.

They were an interesting couple, but the picture of happiness these days. Greg, a Bud Light-loving, NASCAR-watching, camo-as-every-day-wear midwestern man, was as square as they came, but apparently that was the shape of Penny's peg. Sadie shuddered. Okay, that was a terrible analogy.

"Do you really think I need a disguise?"

Penny nodded, reaching into the pocket of her jacket. "You need to match this press pass I whipped up for ya."

Sadie groaned. "This seems way too official. Are we going to get in trouble? I'm trying to lie low. I could just wait for you to tell me what happens."

"Or watch online like a normal person, but what fun is that? Now, chop chop, I made it as easy as I could for you."

Sadie studied the picture. It was her with red hair and different glasses.

"How did you...make this?"

"Artificial Intelligence!" Penny said, beaming. "You'd be shocked what I can do with AI. It writes better than Randall, that's for sure. Now, one of the wigs has an attached scarf. It's easy to put on," Penny said. She pulled into the national park visitor center parking lot, where the press was already assembling. "You better hurry, we gotta go in."

A few minutes later, Penny deemed her ready to go. She was wearing the wig with the scarf, round tortoiseshell glasses instead of her normal square ones—which meant she wasn't going to be able to see any information presented at the front of the room, but Penny insisted that was beside the point—and she'd been helped into a more appropriate blazer instead of her ratty sweater, her sling carefully adjusted. Penny clipped the press pass to Sadie's pocket and grinned. "Follow my lead!" She trilled, turning away to grab her camera bag and notebook.

"I feel pretty plain compared to you," Sadie murmured as they hastened to the door. Penny's look today was giving baby goth, from the Doc Martens to the black cape to the winged eyeliner.

"Not everyone can serve," Penny said, snapping her fingers. At the door to the visitor center, she held up her press pass. "Local press here," she said to the stern security officer.

He glanced at the pass, then Sadie's, which she held with quivering fingers, and then waved them through. Penny winked at her. In the large, open room with a view of the Tetons out the big window, Penny surveyed the gathered crowd.

"Gotta get to the front," she said, elbowing her way through the crowd. "Local press," she said, batting her eyes at a man in an NBC windbreaker. He backed off.

They took their seats in the front row, and Sadie sunk down in hers. "This was a bad idea. Everyone's looking at us."

"Oh, of course they are," Penny said airily. "But we won't be the stars of the show." Penny studied her notebook, which was covered in a rainbow scrawl Sadie couldn't discern.

"You still write in rainbow, even though you're in your Goth Period?"

Penny grinned. "Manic pixie nightmare, remember? You can never guess what I'm doing next."

"Why isn't Randall here, anyway?"

"His girlfriend's sister's daughter's best friend needed a dad-like-figure to attend Donuts with Dads at school, and I volunteered him, of course." Then she shushed her. Law enforcement was filing into the room. And Detective Will Nolan, who apparently warranted a position on the task force, was looking right at her.

Chapter Eleven

"Red alert, red alert," Sadie whispered, looking anywhere but at Will, whose brilliant blue eyes were boring into her.

Penny looked from Sadie to Will, then shrugged. "What's he gonna do? Stop the whole press conference? The big boys are here. He can yell at you later. Which is my least favorite thing he does to you." She glared at him.

What Sadie wouldn't give for an ounce of Penny's overconfidence. What could Will do? Have her kicked out. Have her arrested. Humiliate her on national television. Something she hadn't even thought of yet.

But before she could worry too much about it, the press conference started.

It was pretty humdrum stuff.

All the stakeholders were introduced, from the local to federal level. It was stressed, and overstressed, that everyone was working together to solve the crime. They acknowledged there were a lot of questions, and intense interest in the case, both locally and nationally, but they would be taking their time on the investigation to do it right. They did have a little information to release, though.

They had a timeline.

Most of it, Sadie knew. The polling place opened at seven. Volunteers arrived at six to set up. The morning had been steady with voters. Then it got interesting.

According to the mustachioed spokesperson, at 9:54 A.M., an election judge at the front door—"Kamari," Sadie whispered to Penny, who nodded—noticed smoke in the vestibule.

"They immediately evacuated the voters that were in line and pulled the fire alarm. The security system shows the alarm was pulled at 9:55 A.M. Multiple calls were made to 911 in the next few minutes as the election judges, who did an incredible job, evacuated the building."

Penny snorted, and a few nearby reporters looked at her in reprimand. "Someone *died*," she hissed. "How good of a job did they do?"

The spokesperson droned on like he hadn't heard her. "Simultaneously as the fire was being called in to dispatch, the 911 center received a bomb threat to the polling place."

Sadie sat up straight. That was news to her.

"Firefighters entered the building at 10:01 A.M. The closest fire station is less than three minutes away. Their response time was outstanding. Upon entry, they were notified by a late-evacuating voter that they had found a person deceased inside."

Late-evacuating. She'd never been described that way. She felt her face flame. That was her. He was talking about her.

"Further, the evacuee stated she believed the person had suffered non-fire-related injuries. With this information, firefighters implemented crime scene tactics and tried to preserve the scene as much as possible while containing and controlling the fire."

"The fire was controlled at 11:31 A.M. and mostly

contained to the vestibule area of the building. At that point, investigators entered and identified one deceased individual. As has been reported, that individual was Wade Fisher, fifty-seven, of Jackson. A candidate for Mayor."

The spokesperson paused. "After the crime scene was thoroughly investigated according to protocols, Mr. Fisher was transported to the Teton County Coroner for an autopsy. That information is pending release, and we do not expect to release it for several days." He checked his notes. "And that's all the information we're planning to release at this time, though we will take questions."

The room burst into activity, reporters jumping out of their seats and waving their arms. Penny rolled her eyes, then stood lazily.

"The *Journal*," the spokesperson said, and everyone quieted down. Penny posed for a second, then asked her question, which was concise, pointed, and perfect.

Sadie watched her in awe. She was seriously lucky with her friends.

Of course, the spokesperson rewarded her with, "no comment at this time."

Penny sighed and sat down. "Cowards," she said under her breath.

"How'd you do that?" Sadie whispered.

"Local always gets first question," Penny winked. "These folks haven't been local recently enough to remember."

The spokesperson, for all they said they would take questions, answered virtually none. The only information Sadie gleaned was that yes, they had several suspects identified and were pursuing those leads. Sadie had a question, though, and no one else asked it.

"Will you ask a question for me?" Sadie whispered to Penny, who shook her head.

"I don't get another one. Ask it yourself?"

That seemed like a recipe for disaster. Will hadn't taken his eyes off her the entire press conference. Sadie could feel sweat dripping down her back, and her arm was aching. She needed to take a pain pill, but they were in the coat she'd left in Penny's car. The question was so *obvious*, though. And when was she going to get a chance to ask it?

As the questions dwindled and the task force started to shift from foot to foot with impatience, Sadie stood on shaking legs. The spokesperson looked right at her and pointed.

"The *Journal*, second question."

Shit.

Sadie pulled it together, though. She'd played tougher roles than this in high school drama. She needed to play a character. Ace reporter, Sadie Moose. Though, best not to say her name.

She cleared her throat. It felt like ages had passed but it had only been a second. "Uh, thank you. With the tight timeline, is it possible you're looking at two separate crimes?"

All the eyes on her swiveled to the spokesperson, who paused. "That's...a possibility we're exploring," he said. Sadie sat down quickly, trying to hide.

"Good one," Penny said approvingly.

There was another burst of activity, reporters jockeying to ask another question, but he held up his hands. "That was the last one. We'll have another press conference tomorrow at noon if we have new information to share." And with that, they filed out of the room. Thank goodness. It appeared she'd avoided a Will Nolan talking to, at least for now. Penny glad-handed with the reporters, and then she and Sadie headed for the door. Penny was under a deadline and Sadie wanted out of the wig. She was due for a pain pill and a nap. She checked her watch. *Dang.* Before she could nap, she needed to meet with her new lawyer.

"Sadie Moose," a stern voice said from behind her, and she froze.

Shit. She was caught.

* * *

Sadie turned slowly, a sheepish smile pasted on her face. Will frowned at her. He opened his mouth, and she prepared for the dressing down, but a woman interrupted him, appearing at his side.

"Sadie Moose?" The woman asked. She was a white woman in her forties, with brown hair pulled back from her face in a low ponytail. She wore business attire, with a badge around her neck on a chain. She opened it, showing her a brief look at her ID. "Wyoming Department of Criminal Investigations Special Agent Alice Cooke," she said, snapping her badge closed. "I've been hoping to speak with you." She eyed Will and a wide-eyed Penny. "Alone."

"Sadie never talks without a lawyer," Will said, and Sadie glared at him. He didn't need her to speak for her. Even if that was...mostly true.

"I don't want to speak about the case," Agent Cooke said. "I've heard of you and want to chat. I promise if I want to delve into case stuff, I'll let you know ahead of time."

That sounded reasonable. And though Sadie knew cops built an aura of affability and truthfulness to build a case against you, Agent Cooke had an air of straightforwardness about her.

"Sure," Sadie said with a pointed look at Will. "I'd be happy to speak to you alone. Would you mind walking with me to my friend's car? I'm due for a pill," she gestured to her arm. Agent Cooke pulled a face.

"Ouch. Yeah, I'll walk along."

"I'll be behind you," Penny said. "Absolutely not eaves-dropping."

Sadie and Agent Cooke took off across the parking lot. Sadie glanced behind her. "She's for sure listening."

Agent Cooke shrugged. "That's okay. Nothing I'm saying is confidential, I just wanted to get out of there. And introduce myself. I am the lead investigator for this case, but that's not why I want to talk to you."

"Though I need to give a statement, still."

"I've been assured you will."

"I will," Sadie promised. "I'm meeting with my lawyer later today."

They paused, waiting for a news van to drive by. Agent Cooke turned to look her in the eye. She was only a little taller than Sadie. "I've worked on cases across the state," she began. "And in my time, I've run into a few people like you."

Sadie didn't know if that sounded like a good thing, though Agent Cooke's tone was affable. "There's a geologist down in Gillette that beats me every time. She's incredible."

Sadie stared at her.

"And then a professor in Cheyenne at UW. She teaches history, but her hobby is genealogy. I don't...actually know how she puts everything together to solve cases. Cold cases! Without DNA evidence. Honestly, I think she might be psychic. I've never believed in that stuff. But it's like she's getting messages from the dead. I can't explain it."

"I don't think I understand," Sadie said, confused.

"I've heard of baker sleuths, but I've never worked with one. This is something whispered about at conferences, you know? No classes at the academy on you folks. Anyway, is there some-thing special about baking that helps you solve cases?"

"She knows everyone in town," Penny said, dropping the pretense that she wasn't listening. "And anyone she doesn't know ends up coming to the bakery. I think that's the trick. Plus, her cookies? They can get anyone to talk."

Sadie swatted at Penny with her good arm. "Shush, I'm trying to work this out."

Agent Cooke held up her hands in surrender. "I'm just saying. I've heard about you, and I want you to know that I'm your ally." She reached into her pocket to pull out a card. "This has all my numbers on it. And my personal email. Text me, whatever. If you have a hunch, I want to know about it."

Sadie took the card and stared at it. "You're...not going to try to stop me?"

"Oh, I should," Agent Cooke sighed. "This is one of the most serious cases I've worked on in my career. And I know you have an emotional connection. But I've learned it's not worth telling an amateur sleuth to back off. So, as much as I can swing it, consider me your partner. Now. Do you have any hunches you want to share?"

Sadie opened her mouth, then closed it. "I...I'm still learning about the case. But I can assure you Paige didn't do this. She doesn't have a motive."

Agent Cooke nodded. "I hear you. Thanks for that vote of confidence for her. She seems like a great woman. Inspiring."

Sadie gulped. "She is. Wait, Agent Cooke, are you serious about this?"

"As a heart attack," Agent Cooke said. "And call me Alice. As long as none of these other knuckleheads are around." Her phone buzzed on her belt, and she reached for it. "I have to take this. I'll see you soon, Sadie. Nice talking to you both." She waved and turned, walking back to the visitor center.

Penny stared at Sadie. "Did that woman...verify that Jessica Fletchers exist in real life?"

"But they're apparently bakers, geologists, and professors,"

Sadie said, perplexed. "That was the most bizarre conversation I've ever had."

"You need to have more conversations, then," Penny said, wrapping her arm around her and squeezing gently. "Now, I have it on good authority from Robin that you turn into a pumpkin shortly after one, so I need to get you home. Let's go."

Penny dropped her off in front of her house, and Sadie was halfway up her walkway when she realized she was still wearing the wig, though she'd changed her glasses out immediately, a headache forming from the non-prescription ones. She couldn't wait for this meeting to be over so she could lie down. Maybe rest would help settle her racing brain. She felt like she'd learned something important today, but she couldn't put her finger on it. There'd been so much, from the photos to the revelations on Gotham Enterprises to the press conference.

She opened her front door, expecting Tyrone to greet her, but he didn't. She frowned. Maybe he was in the backyard.

There were voices in the kitchen, so she headed that direction.

When she reached the doorway, she froze. Her mom was standing at the kitchen island, talking to someone whose face Sadie couldn't see. She had long blonde hair and a diamond the size of a baseball on her left hand. Robin spotted her, smiling. "Oh, Sadie! You're here. Let me introduce you to your lawyer. Nora Mooney."

Chapter Twelve

Nora turned, a wide grin on her face that quickly turned puzzled. "Did you change your hair?"

Sadie raised her hand to the wig, having forgotten about it again. She pulled it off, sure she looked a mess. "Uh. Long story." She glanced around for a place to put it, then hung it on a nearby coat hook. It looked like Cousin It cascading down the wall. She turned back to Nora and her mother, who were watching her with amusement. "Wait. How do you know what my hair looks like?"

Nora blushed. Actually blushed. Prettily. "Oh, I've seen your picture in the paper! And I've heard so much about you from your mom already. I'm messing this all up, but I'm so glad to meet you." She hopped off the stool and offered her hand. Sadie shook it, reluctantly. How was this happening to her?

"Sadie, what's wrong with you?" Her mother asked. "Why are you acting so funny?"

Sadie tried to shake it off. Agent Cooke thought she was a Jessica Fletcher. She needed to act like one. "Just a long day already," she said. "Sorry. Wonderful to meet you, thanks for helping me out with this."

"Of course," Nora chirped. "Now, let's settle in so you can tell me what's going on and how best I can help you."

Robin led them to the living room and then left to tend to Tyrone.

"Oh, yes, I'm allergic to dogs," Nora said, almost embarrassed. "I love them, but they make my eyes itch." She gave a little sneeze, as if to emphasize it.

Sadie blanched. "Yeah...Tyrone's been on all these couches. Would we be better off outside?"

"Oh no, I'll be okay," Nora said. She pulled a portfolio out of her slim briefcase and propped it up in her lap. "Now, first, let me introduce myself. I'm an independent lawyer based out of Cheyenne, but I've recently moved to Jackson to run a philanthropic organization. This is good for you in that currently, you'd be my only client. But there could be drawbacks. Not being part of a large firm, if we need to consult with other specialty lawyers, it could get expensive."

Sadie stared at her. This was. Too much.

Jessica Fletcher. That geologist and professor that impressed Agent Cooke so much. You can do this.

"Okay," Sadie said. "That's...okay. I don't think this is going to end up being that big of a deal. I need to give a statement and can't use my normal guy, Mateo, because he's wrapped up in it."

Nora nodded earnestly. "Absolutely. I have extensive experience in criminal law if it does come to that, though. Now, can I answer any other questions about me?"

Sadie had questions. Boy did she.

"How...did my dad find you?"

Nora grinned. "Oh, Arlo and I have a mutual friend. When he heard you needed some help, he asked me to contact Arlo."

Sadie gulped. Ah, here it was, the reason her dad had been so sly earlier. "Can I...ask who the mutual friend is?"

"Of course! You know him, too, maybe? He's about your age and he's from here. Merritt West?"

Sadie gritted her teeth. "I'm acquainted with him, yes."

"Isn't he the best? I adore him!"

"How wonderful," Sadie said, trying so hard not to show her true feelings. Merritt had asked his fiancé to contact Sadie's father to help her? She should kick her out right now.

But she needed her help.

And she could deal with Merritt later.

"That all sounds great, Nora. I appreciate this. Do we need to sign anything before I tell you what happened yesterday?"

"It's like you've done this before," Nora joked. When Sadie didn't laugh, she sobered. "Oh, have you done this before?"

"A time or two," Sadie said, not able to keep herself from smiling. Nora was so earnest. So sweet. She was tiny, too, lithe, and athletic, with all that hair and the pretty complexion. She was everything Sadie wasn't. Sadie felt like a big, frumpy blob next to her. A broken one, with the arm. She felt a familiar tightness in her chest and dropped her head back to take a deep, calming breath. Right. Anxiety. That was her anxiety speaking. And anxiety lied, all the time.

"Hey, are you okay?" Nora asked. She put a cool, slim hand on Sadie's. "Can I get you some water or something?"

"Yeah, actually, that would be great," Sadie said. "I need a minute, and then we can get going."

"Are you sure? Because I could come back later."

Sadie assured her it was okay, and by the time Nora returned with a glass of ice water and a plate of cheese and crackers she was sure her mom had put together, Sadie had gotten a grip. This pleasant woman was here to help her—for a hefty fee, according to the paperwork Sadie signed—but she wasn't responsible for Merritt's actions.

Nora asked pointed questions, and a lot of them, but eventually she was happy with the statement Sadie was prepared to give. She detailed what Sadie could expect when she gave her statement, and when Nora would step in, and then their meeting was over. After promising she would text Sadie as soon as she'd scheduled the police interview, she left, and Robin bundled Sadie into bed with a heat pad and no phone.

"You need proper rest," Robin insisted as she took it away. "No electronics. I'll be back in two hours."

And though Sadie wanted to protest, she found it felt good, to be taken care of. To be watched after. So she gave in, letting her body relax, letting the heat take the ache out of her arm. She let all the worries slip away. They'd be there when she awoke.

* * *

Sadie woke up knowing that it was time.

She needed to confront Merritt. She was sick of carrying around the hurt he'd caused her like a millstone around her neck. It was the monkey on her back, the chip on her shoulder, the burden she had to carry. And she was done with it.

She dragged herself out of bed, blinking at the time on her bedside clock. Four in the afternoon. She felt like she'd slept the entire night, but it had only been a couple hours. She splashed water on her face—awkwardly, one handed—in the bathroom, then moseyed out into the living room, almost tripping over Tyrone, who'd been sleeping outside her closed door. She reached down to pet him, apologizing for kicking him.

He looked at her morosely.

Sadie had recently heard that dogs didn't understand mistakes, so if you tripped over them, they thought you kicked them on purpose. This guilt propelled her to the kitchen, where she grabbed a handful of treats from his treat jar and fed them to him, not even making him do tricks to earn them.

On the kitchen island was her phone, along with a note from her mom.

I hope you slept a long time. Don't check the news. Nothing's happened, but the rhetoric is getting worse. Saw there's a vigil for Wade tonight at six at town square. Might be a good place to hunt for suspects. XO, Mom.

Sadie quirked a smile. So supportive of her efforts. She picked up her phone, sliding onto a barstool at the island. She pointedly didn't check the news but scrolled through her text messages.

From Kendall:

> Vigil tonight at six, pick you up at 5:45?

From Gavin:

> Heard we're going to a candlelight vigil to question people. I'll bring snacks.

From Penny:

> Randall saw the press conference and wanted me to ask you to sign on as a stringer. He can offer an incredibly low per word rate plus minimal mileage. I wouldn't take it if I was you.

From Kamari:

> I took Tyrone for a run while you were napping. Don't let him talk you into treats, I already gave him plenty.

Sadie looked at Tyrone, who'd sprawled down under her. She rubbed his head with her foot. "You little con artist." He winked at her.

Sadie replied to the messages, cementing plans, turning down Randall's gracious offer to become an independent reporter, and thanking Kamari for taking Tyrone out. Then she took a deep breath, scrolling her list of text messages to find a thread that hadn't been active for over a year.

There he was. Merritt West. She'd never blocked him. He didn't answer texts when he was working. She didn't even know if he still had the same phone number. New life, new fiancé, new number, who dis? But before she could back out, she sent a message.

We need to talk.

She stared at it for a moment, then jumped when the three dots that indicated he was typing showed up. *Shit.* She'd been positive this wouldn't work.

About time. Want me to come by?

Sadie glanced around the apple-themed kitchen her mom had decorated in the nineties that Sadie had never updated. At this point, the red apple drawer pulls, apple clock, and apple border were nearing kitschy, not outdated. Could she have him in her house? Everywhere she looked she had a memory of him, from growing up as kids, and then from their short-lived love affair. She blushed, looking at the counter. There'd been one night...

Right.

Not here.

She sent a quick text, then got up to get ready. She had

about an hour and a half before the vigil started. Plenty of time to meet with Merritt, clear the air, ask some questions, and move on. As friends, maybe. Or maybe as nothing. Somebody that she used to know.

Sadie left the house, ensuring she locked up behind her and set the alarm. With the way friends popped in and out all day, she rarely worried about it, but Sully's warning rang through her brain. The killer might not know she hadn't seen them. She shivered. It was only three blocks to the brewery where she was meeting Merritt, but it was getting dark.

She hurried the entire way, glancing over her shoulder frequently.

She made it without incident, though, feeling silly when the lights of the brewery came in view. She slowed as she approached it. The multi-story building was buzzing with activity. It was chilly, but the heaters on the decks meant plenty of diners were enjoying the crisp night. And out on the lawn, where in warmer weather kids played yard games while their parents watched, sipping their fresh brews, the fire pit was lit, Adirondack chairs around it.

Only one was occupied, by a man with broad shoulders and a shaggy head of blonde hair, which glinted in the firelight. As she got closer, his hazel gaze met hers.

And the world melted away.

Chapter Thirteen

He stood, and she drifted closer to him.

Would they hug? Was that appropriate? In the end, Sadie stood awkwardly while he leaned in, brushing his lips across her cheek. He smelled like crisp fall air, hops, and vanilla. She couldn't explain it. He'd always smelled...*warm* to her. Then he was pulling back, gesturing at a chair.

She sat.

"Can I get you a drink?"

She shook her head. "No, I'm on pain meds." She raised her sling an inch, then winced. He looked concerned.

"How is your arm?"

"Broken," Sadie said shortly. "I should get a cast tomorrow. At least I didn't need surgery."

"That's something." He played with his glass, which was empty. He'd apparently beat her there by some time. Or he'd pounded his beer. "I kept coming here," he said suddenly. "Hoping I'd see you. Instead, Nash glowered and refused to talk every time."

"He's a loyal friend," Sadie said honestly. She put her good hand out to the fire, warming it. She should've worn gloves. The vigil was going to be cold. It was cloudy, with a slight breeze. She could smell snow on it.

"So am I," Merritt said, his voice shaky. "Everything I've done, I've done for you. And you wouldn't even talk to me."

"Did you try?" Sadie said, confused. "Besides showing up here? When did you try to talk? You know where I live. You know where I work. You know my number, apparently. And what does that mean, everything you've done? You have a lot to explain."

"I do," Merritt said, holding up his hands in surrender. "And I'm willing to do so if you're willing to listen."

Sadie swallowed hard. Was she ready to listen? There was so much going on right now. She'd found a dead body yesterday. Her best friend was the top suspect. Her arm was broken. Was now the time to hear the story? She checked her watch. "Honestly, Merritt. I don't have a lot of time. I have a vigil to attend. Kendall's picking me up in ten. Is that enough time?"

"It should be."

She gestured for him to go on. "Then do it."

"Sadie Moose?"

Sadie turned toward the voice, and a bright light blinded her. She threw up her hand to shield her eyes, then sprang up. "No comment!"

The reporter gestured at the videographer to keep rolling. "Are you Paige Gates's best friend? We have questions! Do you think she did it?"

Sadie gritted her teeth. "Paige Gates-*Ortiz*," she corrected.

"Are you her friend?" The reporter asked, ignoring her correction. "Tell me about her! Is she capable of murder?"

"She said no comment," Merritt said from beside her. He

reached over, pulling Sadie's coat hood up over her head, and she glanced at him gratefully, burrowing beneath it.

The camera swiveled to him. "Who are you?" The reporter asked. "Do you know Paige? Do you think she murdered Wade Fisher?"

Merritt groaned. "No comment from me either. Now leave, please."

"We can be here if we want," the reporter said, her voice snotty.

"No, you can't," a gruff voice said from behind them. "Move out to the sidewalk."

Thank goodness for Nash.

"Says who?" The videographer asked.

"Me. The manager of the brewery. Want me to get the owners on the line? I own twenty percent, so I only need two other owners for a majority vote. One is at the bar right now and he's been drinking since two."

"Fine," the reporter said. "But we're trying to find out what's going on here. This town isn't very friendly."

"Imagine," Merritt said quietly to Sadie. "Imagine coming into town and assaulting people on the streets to spill their secrets and then complaining that the town isn't friendly."

Sadie couldn't help but smile. She watched Nash herd them over to the sidewalk. "Now don't bug my customers," he said. He came back to them. The camera was still pointed their way. "Sorry about that. Also, glad you two are talking. Does this mean I can speak to Merritt now?" He looked at Sadie expectantly.

Sadie rolled her eyes. "I've gotten zero story out of him, but yeah. I suppose so."

Nash pulled Merritt into a bear hug. "Hey brother," he said. "Good to have you home."

"Good to be home," Merritt said, thumping his back.

Sadie stared. "Home?"

Merritt turned his gaze to hers. Their eyes met. "Yeah. I'm back. For good."

* * *

In the back of Kendall's car, Kamari in the front passenger seat, Sadie turned to Merritt. "Okay, so apparently, we don't have time for the full story. But tell me one thing."

He pursed his lips, thinking.

"Was it you?" Sadie asked, unable to wait. "Are you Gotham Enterprises? All of it, the fake reality TV show, the vans, the free money, all of it?"

"Yes," he said. "It's me. Though not really me anymore. I handed over the reins along with the money."

Sadie gritted her teeth. "Right. To Nora. Who's sweet, by the way."

"Isn't she?" Merritt said, smiling. "She's a great fit."

Sadie tried not to let that punch her too hard in the gut.

"Wow," Kendall said from the front seat, meeting Sadie's eyes in the rearview mirror.

Kamari turned around to stare down Merritt. "The balls on this one," she sniffed.

Merritt shifted uncomfortably, looking confused. "What? She's a great fit as the CEO of Gotham. She can sniff out a scam from a mile away but her heart's in the right place. She's going to give away a ton of money. My money." Sadie poked him in the side, and he shifted away from her. "Ouch! What's going on? Why is everyone mad at me? You told me I should give away all my money, and I'm doing it! I'm basically a pauper now!"

Sadie narrowed her eyes at him. "A pauper wouldn't buy

their fiancé a diamond ring so big it's visible from the International Space Station."

Kendall snorted from the front seat and Kamari put up her hand for a high five, which Sadie gave her, eyes never leaving Merritt.

Merritt's eyes were wide. Then he started laughing. Full body chuckles. He threw back his head and laughed and laughed. Kendall pulled the car over to turn and look at him. All three women stared at him, dumbfounded.

Finally, he calmed, wiping his eyes. He pulled out his phone, swiping, then held up the screen.

Sadie gulped.

It was Nora. Wrapped around a tall, dark, and handsome man, who smiled at her adoringly. They were in front of a chalet in the mountains, the trees golden and heavy with leaves, the Tetons in the background. He scrolled down with his thumb, revealing the caption.

Only six months until this amazing man makes me his wife! 🤍 🤍 🤍 *I love you, chicken butt!* 😜

And she'd tagged @AricDanza. As in entrepreneur Aric Danza. Who lived in Jackson.

"Oh, sugar cookies," Kendall cursed under her breath. She put her hands over her eyes. "I was there, though. I saw you! She was all over you!"

"Where? When?"

"This summer! You were at Elk & Olive, and I was walking by..."

Merritt squinted, trying to think. "Yeah. I came outside to say hey, and you...ran away?"

Sadie shook her head. "This is too much. To be clear... you're telling me Nora Mooney isn't your fiancé?"

"No! She wanted to move to Jackson and get out of law, so I interviewed her to take over Gotham this summer. We celebrated at Elk & Olive when she accepted the job. She...maybe she had her arm through mine? We're friends! Seriously, only friends. Aric's a scary ass dude, please don't get me in trouble with him."

Kamari snorted. She had her phone out and was scrolling Aric's Instagram profile. "The man is ripped. He's not lying. About her being his fiancé, either. I'm deep into last year and he posts a lot of pictures of him and Nora together."

Sadie rubbed her hands over her eyes.

"This is why y'all have been mad at me?" Merritt asked. "This is why you blocked me on IG?"

Sadie nodded. "Yes. Yes, this is why." She uncovered her face. "Actually, no. It's not the only reason. Why all the incognito shit with the fake show and stuff?"

He stared at her. "I named it *Gotham Enterprises*. And aren't you some sort of detective?"

"Apparently not a very good one," Sadie sighed. Should she have figured that out?

There was silence, and then Kendall started giggling. And then Kamari started. And then Sadie joined in. Merritt didn't.

"I'm glad y'all feel better," he said grumpily.

"So much better," Sadie said, sighing. She was filled with relief. She patted Merritt's leg. "I still need more answers, but that's enough for now. We're going to be late for our vigil."

Kendall pulled the car back out into the road. She looked at Merritt in the rearview mirror. "Welcome back to the crew, Batman."

* * *

After the encounter with the press at the brewery, Sadie was nervous to attend the vigil, but it appeared the press at this event was more well behaved, filming from a distance. Sadie wondered how long they would stick around. After all, there were other interesting election-related stories nationally. Protesters at the counts in Arizona. A surprisingly tight race resulting in a recount in a previously non-swing seat. But even those two big stories weren't as exciting as a bomb, a murder, and a rival as top suspect. Sadie had to concede that.

They joined the crowd tentatively, looking for faces turned to them in anger, but Sadie thought most of the mourners were like her, unfortunately. Looky loos. She spotted Nancy Fisher and turned away, hoping the woman wouldn't see her. What if she noticed the man from the photos with her? That could only add to her conspiracy theory.

Which reminded her.

She punched Merritt lightly in the arm to get his attention, and he rubbed it. "I'm getting beat up today. Please stop poking and punching me."

"Sorry," Sadie said, patting his arm in apology. "I forget how soft you are."

He glared at her.

"Anyway. I saw some pictures of you meeting with Paige. What the heck was that all about? What'd you do to get her to promise not to tell me?"

His gaze darkened. "Pictures? How?"

"I'll show them to you later," Sadie promised. "But Nancy Fisher, Wade's mom, had them taken. I'm guessing she had a private eye or someone follow Paige. She's convinced that her being associated with Gotham means you colluded with her on her campaign."

He snorted. "No. Nothing I did had anything to do with Paige's campaign. And the meeting was about an affordable housing project that's in its infancy. Nora met with everyone on the council, it's not a secret. I didn't even know they were meeting when I dropped by to see Nora."

"Was Paige mad?"

"Absolutely enraged, and I didn't know why. As soon as I got there, she left."

"She never told me," Sadie said.

"Did you ask her why?"

"She won't talk to me," she said sadly. "She's under surveillance and doesn't want me roped into any more trouble."

"I'm sure she has her reasons," Merritt said. "Paige never does anything without a reason."

That was true. "I have so many questions, but I can't ask her."

"Means you have to ask other people," Kendall said from beside her. "And that's why we're here to help. Who else do you suspect?"

Sadie sighed. She had zero other suspects. She wanted to ask questions of Wade's wife, Madison, and his campaign manager, who she didn't even know the name of. But so far, she hadn't heard one thing that would make someone else a suspect. No wonder the police were focused on Paige.

Raised voices from the heart of the event, where the picture of Wade and the candles were centered, caught their attention.

Sadie stood on her tiptoes, trying to see over the crowd.

"How dare you show up here?" A loud voice screeched. The crowd shifted, and Sadie could finally see.

It was Madison Fisher, being physically restrained from attacking a petite blonde woman, who smirked at her.

"You bitch!" Madison screamed.

The press, formerly polite, circled in like vultures in for the kill. The other woman stepped closer to Madison and said something that caused Madison's face to crumple, sobs heaving from her. The woman turned on her heel and walked away.

Sadie glanced at her companions. "Kendall, you watch Madison. Kamari, I need you to identify the campaign manager for me." She looked at Merritt. "You and me? We follow that woman."

Chapter Fourteen

They caught her right before she climbed into her vehicle, a silver G-Class Mercedes SUV, informally known as a G-Wagon.

"Ma'am," Sadie called. The woman looked over her shoulder, her frantic features smoothing out when she realized Sadie wasn't carrying a camera or microphone. She peered at her and Merritt.

"Yes?"

"I wanted to check on you. Are you okay?" Sadie asked, casting about internally for an angle to build camaraderie.

The woman relaxed. "I'm. I'm not, but thanks for asking. No one's asked me that yet." Her face crumpled, and she sagged against the car. Sadie glanced at Merritt, who shrugged. Not a helpful sidekick, that one.

"Sadie?" She turned, finding Gavin looking at her with confusion, a cooler bag slung over his shoulder. Only he could make that look cool and not like he was headed to his kid's soccer practice with orange slices and Goldfish.

"Gavin!" Sadie waved him over. He approached slowly, frowning at Merritt.

"I thought we hated you," he said, glaring at him.

"The jury's still out," Sadie said, shrugging, "but we have an informal truce for now."

"Huh. Well, in that case, sup, my name's Gavin."

They shook hands.

"What's that amazing smell?" The woman asked, her tears slowing some as she sniffed the air.

"Gavin's a chef and he brought snacks," Sadie explained. "I bet he'd share with you. Are you hungry?"

"Starved," she said. She blinked. "Who are you, again?"

They made introductions all around. The blonde woman's name was Ashley. Or Ashleigh, Sadie corrected internally, when she specified, "with an eigh." Sadie guessed she was only twenty or so, a white woman with model good looks, designer clothes, and an extremely expensive vehicle. Ashleigh opened the back hatch of her G-Wagon and invited Gavin to place his snacks there. They then gathered for one of the most unusual picnics of Sadie's life.

"So," Sadie said, when her little plate was full of bacon-wrapped dates, caprese skewers, and huckleberry BBQ drumettes. "Can I ask what your relationship with Wade was?"

Ashleigh hiccupped, shoved a date into her mouth, and then wiped her eyes again. "I loved him," she said around the mouthful, then swallowed. "Sorry, I haven't eaten all day. I've been too upset."

Gavin, Merritt, and Sadie looked at each other.

"Yes," Ashleigh said, sighing. "I loved him like that. We've been together for over a year."

"I'm so sorry for your loss," Gavin said, recovering before Sadie did. "No wonder you're so upset. And it was a secret? So, you're not getting any sympathy." He reached into the cooler and pulled out a foil tray, peeling off the lid. "Take a brownie, sweetheart."

"Thank you," Ashleigh said, sniffling, reaching in for one. "And I know what you're thinking. I'm the worst. But he and Madison had a terrible relationship! She's awful to him. He promised me he was going to leave her for good once the election was over."

Woah. That was huge. And, finally—a motive for someone to kill Wade? Although...if you were someone's spouse, would you choose such a public place to murder them? Wouldn't it be easier to do at home? In a much less obvious way?

"And now I get nothing," Ashleigh said, her voice cracking. "He promised me a trip to Bali for my twenty-first birthday!"

Merritt grimaced, and Sadie elbowed him discreetly. They needed Ashleigh on their side. He shoved a date in his mouth. Good. He needed to keep quiet.

"I'm so sorry," Sadie said, patting Ashleigh's knee. "Is that what the fight with Madison was about? How awful. You were there to pay your respects."

"And to get them," Ashleigh said, bitingly. "But his friends pretended they didn't know who I was. And then Madison flew off the handle and told me to go. How dare she. She didn't even win Miss Arizona. She was the first runner up and then the actual winner got in trouble for explicit pictures and Madison inherited the title. She wasn't in the top ten at Miss America."

Sadie blinked at her, but Ashleigh wasn't done. "I won Miss Teen Nevada all on my own, fair and square," she said proudly. "And I was in the top ten at Miss Teen USA."

Gavin coughed into his elbow in a way that made Sadie think it was actually a laugh, but Sadie didn't find any of this funny. What a sleazeball Wade had been. He'd traded in his pageant queen wife for a teen pageant queen mistress. Dirtbag behavior.

"Who do you think killed him?" Merritt asked, apparently unable to keep his mouth shut any longer.

Ashleigh blinked. "That town council lady, right? That's what everyone's saying?"

"I'm pretty confident she didn't," Sadie said, trying to keep the bite out of her voice. "Did Wade have any other enemies?"

She sat up a little straighter. "Wait. Y'all aren't cops, are you?"

"No, no," Sadie assured her. "Just curious."

"Huh. Because I've been thinking about starting a podcast. What do you think? Like *Only Murders in the Building* but without the two old guys, only me, talking about the tragedy I'm going through."

"Uh...that sounds interesting," Sadie said brightly. "You'd need a lot of ideas for that, though. Like other theories, right? Of the murder?"

Ashleigh considered that. "Okay, you're right. I need to think about this more. Well. He and his campaign manager, Elijah, fought a lot."

"What about Madison?" Gavin asked.

"She's a real bitch, so maybe? And now she gets the money, so...yeah, sure." Ashleigh's face crumpled. "And I get nothing. Ugh! Should I try selling my story to a magazine? There are a lot of news vans in town. I was trying to avoid them because Wade always told me to stay discreet, but he's not here anymore, is he? And who's going to make my car payment now?"

Sadie patted her arm. "I'm sure you can trade in the Mercedes for something economical and come out on top."

Ashleigh stared at her. "I mean my Porsche. This old thing is paid for."

Right. The "old thing" was a two-year-old $200,000 car. Sadie was starting to not like Ashleigh much. But she was a kid, going through trauma, that had a lot of growing up to do. She needed to be gentle with her.

"Can you tell us what Elijah and Wade fought about?" Merritt asked, distracting her.

Ashleigh flipped her hair and set down her plate. "Money. Donors. Policies. Me. Elijah was always trying to make Wade smaller than he was. Less loud, less passionate, less...everything."

"Then why did he stick with him? He could've hired someone else." Gavin said. He was packing up the empty dishes, all their bellies full. Kamari and Kendall were going to lose their minds when they found out Miss Teen Nevada ate their share.

"I dunno, they were besties or something," Ashleigh said. She had her phone out and was scrolling. They were losing her.

"Hey, can I text you my number?" Sadie asked. "In case you want to workshop your idea with me?"

"What idea?"

"The podcast."

"Oh, right." Ashleigh looked bored.

"Or, if you need to talk to someone. Do you have a lot of friends in town?"

Ashleigh pulled a face. "No. And what am I supposed to do now? I wonder how long his credit card will work? Will it get me back to Vegas, you think?"

Sadie grimaced. "It might? But, if you need someone local, please. Let me give you my number."

Ashleigh rattled off hers and Sadie sent her quick hello text. They stepped back and Ashleigh shut up the SUV, getting in and waving as she pulled away.

"You're a nice person," Gavin said to Sadie. "She's absolutely going to call you in the middle of the night crying."

Sadie shrugged. "She probably will. And I'll help her if I can. But also, now I have an opening to get more information."

"Strategery," Merritt said in his best George W. Bush voice, and Gavin chuckled.

"I'm glad we don't hate you anymore," he said.

"Trial period," Sadie reminded them. "Now let's go find KitKat so you can explain why you didn't bring them dinner."

* * *

Gavin dragged his feet, but they eventually found the two in the crowd, which had returned to its earlier somber tone, the media again retreating to the outskirts.

"Oh good, you're here. I'm starving," Kendall said, pawing at Gavin's cooler playfully.

Kamari gestured across the park at a short, balding white man blowing his nose into a white handkerchief. "Elijah Stanton, Wade's campaign manager. I've been watching him. He's not doing much."

Sadie thanked her, then left Gavin to deliver the bad news about the snacks, having spotted Madison standing alone. She flinched when she heard Kendall's outraged shriek behind her. Gavin would pay for that.

Madison didn't see her coming, so Sadie was standing right next to her when she spoke.

"Mrs. Fisher?"

Madison turned to her, her neutral face immediately twisting into a frown. "You!" she said. "Why are you here?"

Sadie gulped. "I wanted to extend my condolences. I'm so sorry."

Madison scoffed. "I'm sure you're not."

"I am. I know we were political rivals, but I'm very sorry for all this. This must be so hard on you." Sadie remembered seeing Madison when she walked out of the burning building, her face contorted, tears streaming down her face as she tried over and over again to call her husband. "Pick up, pick up!" She'd said.

Madison sniffled but didn't relent. "You're friends with his *murderer*. I don't want you here. Leave."

Sadie backed away. "I don't want to cause you any more distress, I promise. I'll leave."

"So, you admit she killed him?" Madison said, her voice loud enough people started looking their way.

"I didn't say that," Sadie hissed. "I'm leaving now."

"Leave! Run back to your murderous best friend. So scared she was going to lose the election she *killed* her opponent! My sweet husband! My..." her voice broke off as sobs overcame her. "My Wade!"

Sadie felt the bright lights of the cameras back on her. This was bad. Very bad. She was going to make things harder for Paige, which was the last thing she wanted to do.

"Hurry, get in here," a voice said, and she looked around. Elijah Stanton was in his car, passenger window down, gesturing at her to get in.

And because she maybe wasn't the smartest woman in the world? She got in the car.

* * *

"Just so you know, my friend has a tracker on me and will destroy you if you murder me." Sadie said as Elijah peeled away, the press thankfully missing the move. Her getting caught with him could be hard to explain to Paige.

Though Paige had some of her own explaining to do.

"Noted," Elijah said wryly. "I'm surprised we haven't met. I'm Elijah Stanton, and I'm not a murderer."

"Oh good. I'm Sadie Moose, and neither am I. And also, neither is my best friend, Paige."

Elijah was silent. "If you say so."

Sadie felt like she was going to scream. How did *everyone* believe Paige's guilt? "Seriously? You knew Paige was probably going to win. What did she get out of killing him? There's no motive. She was there with her *infant daughter*! Who she dressed in a matching pantsuit! She wouldn't ruin that moment for anything."

"Self-preservation," Elijah said. "Wade was the king of opposition research. Even if he lost, he wouldn't have given Paige a moment of peace as mayor."

"That's outrageous! I've seen the so-called-oppo Nancy had on Paige and it's completely debunkable."

"You presume that's all he had," he said. "I tried to get him to campaign on merits. I wanted him to...be a man of the people, not a man of the millionaires. But Wade. Wade couldn't ever rein it in."

"So why did you keep working with him?" Elijah had been pulling widening circles around the town square, and now he was getting close to her house.

He sighed heavily. "We grew up together."

"Ah," Sadie said. "Like I grew up with Paige."

"Fair point," he said, tipping his head to her.

"Why did you pick me up, anyway?" Sadie asked.

He shrugged. "Madison can be difficult, and I didn't want her to cause a bigger scene." His voice was thick, and he cleared his throat. "Look at me, still covering for Wade, even now."

Sadie could hear the grief in his voice. He was truly sad he was gone. She felt bad for him. "Hey, my house is up here," Sadie said. "Why don't you drop me off?"

"Sure," he agreed. Sadie told him her address, and he pulled in front of the house.

"I don't suppose you'd tell me what opposition research he had?"

"He kept his cards close to his chest. But even if I knew, I wouldn't tell. My loyalty is to Wade," Elijah said, hanging his head. "Even in death."

"I didn't see you," Sadie said suddenly. "You weren't with Madison, outside. After the fire alarm."

He studied her. "That's true. I didn't vote. I'm not registered here. I live in Idaho."

"So where did you go?"

"Outside, once they got in line for the second time."

Where Claire had gone. An easily verifiable story. Which she would be verifying. Immediately.

Chapter Fifteen

Everyone descended on her house within fifteen minutes of her climbing out of Elijah's car.

None of them were happy.

"You don't just get into some *randos* car!" Kamari insisted. Again. She'd said that a lot of times.

"Especially not a rando associated with a *murder*!" Gavin groused. He'd dropped his stuff off in the guest bedroom, apparently moving in until this was settled.

Merritt hadn't said anything, but he looked very unhappy. Murdery unhappy. She'd really upset them.

"I understand," Sadie said. "But I needed to talk to him anyway, knew Kendall would look up where I was, and planned to text you. I just got distracted. I'm on pain pills, remember?"

"You need a walkie talkie," Kamari groused. "We need to be able to contact you *by voice* every time you do something like this. Which is a lot."

"I love a good walkie talkie," Kendall sighed. She got a stern look on her face. "But we're not letting you off that easy. You're going to pay a price for this." She looked at Kamari. "What do you think? Five?"

"Ten," Kamari said stiffly. "At least."

"Oh, come on. Not ten!" Sadie protested.

"Ten," Kendall said decisively. "You owe us ten TikToks. Of our discretion. Whenever we want."

"Ugh." Sadie hated making TikToks. But she did like how much business they brought the bakery. She could handle the punishment.

"So," Kendall continued. "Since we've experienced two betrayals tonight," she glared at Gavin, who looked chagrined, "I think it's only fair that someone orders pizza."

"I'll do it," Gavin volunteered.

"The menu's on the fridge," Sadie called as he disappeared into the kitchen. There was a knock at the front door, and then Max and Sage ducked in. The two were a hot new item, aside from being coworkers.

"Hey, I thought we hated you," Max said, pointing at Merritt with confusion.

"Did someone say pizza?" Sage asked. "Make sure you get a vegan option." She looked at Merritt. "And who are you and why do we hate you?"

"I'll fill you in," Max promised her.

Gavin groaned from the kitchen, probably thinking about how much sharing with Ashleigh was going to hurt his wallet. "Should we expect anyone else? A marching band? Basketball team? The San Francisco 49ers?"

Sadie didn't answer, knowing he would order extra, anyway.

"Claire and the boys are coming," Kendall called helpfully, and Gavin cursed. Baxter could put away a whole pie on his own. And Slice, Slice, Baby, their favorite pizza joint that was run by a neighborhood kid Sadie and Paige had grown up with, made enormous pies. "Oh!" Sadie said suddenly, sitting up straight. "I have an idea."

She hurried into the kitchen, where Gavin was about to hang up. "Can I talk to them? Who is it? Barry?"

Gavin nodded, handing her his phone.

"Barry? It's Sadie. I need a favor." She paused to listen to him grouse, then cut him off. "No, Barry, a favor like when I pulled an all-nighter to decorate that cake for Tinsley's first birthday after you forgot to order it and I didn't even tell Susan about your mistake?" He was putty in her hands after that.

* * *

It took an hour, but it worked.

While everyone chowed down on pizza in the living room, Sadie sat on her back deck, her coat on and a blanket over her lap. She didn't have an appetite. She wanted a glass of wine, but after the conversation she was hoping to have, a pain pill and dropping off to sleep sounded better.

She heard a crackling noise, and then a beep, and grinned.

"Mastermind, this is Fence. I can't believe you. Over."

It'd been at least twenty years since Paige had spoken her walkie talkie code name over the air. They'd been teenagers, wanting privacy from the family phone in the kitchen, talking to each other late into the night. And then they'd gotten cell phones. They didn't have the same romance the set of pink walkie talkies she'd gotten when she'd turned eight did. She'd given one to Paige, who's childhood home was only two blocks away, and Paige had kept it ever since. Sadie knew that because she'd seen it yesterday morning when she'd been looking for wipes for Luna. It'd been in the hall closet, and it had made her smile. Now, it was a hopefully untraceable way to communicate with her friend. Because she needed some questions answered.

"Fence, Mastermind. After all these years, the nickname finally manifested. Over."

"And I've always been a Fence. You okay?"

Sadie took a deep breath. Was she? "Yeah. You okay?"

There was a long pause, then a crackling. The line was open, but Paige took a moment to speak. "Not really. But I will be. The pizza's delicious by the way."

She appreciated her honesty. And the pizza was good.

"I have questions, but first...guess who's here?"

There was silence for a moment. "I'm afraid to guess."

"Batman."

The reply came quickly. "I swear I didn't tell him anything, I was so mad—"

"You can tell me later," Sadie interrupted. "It's okay. He's trying to explain things. It's not important right now."

"Okay."

"I'm trying to help," Sadie said. "Get you through this. I need information."

"I hope you know what you're doing, Mastermind."

"The name implies I do."

Sadie held her breath in the silence.

"Hit me."

"I saw...Angler tell you something in line. What was it?"

"An insinuation. Put my back up, but nothing I hadn't heard before. Baseless."

"Why'd you get separated from...Picket and Latch?" Sadie really should've brainstormed code words beforehand.

There was no mirth in Paige's voice, though. "Angler. They stopped me."

"Why?"

Paige's voice was small. And not just because it was coming through early-nineties tech. "They threatened me."

"With what?"

"Not with words. Physically. To withdraw. To resign."

Sadie felt her heart beat faster. How dare he. How *dare* he.

"I ripped myself away and ran."

Sadie waited.

"I stumbled. That must have been when I dropped my...tampon."

Despite the tension, Sadie couldn't help but guffaw. She hoped any FBI agent in a listening truck eavesdropping on their conversation dropped their coffee on their keyboard at the perfect code-naming.

"After that, I ran. Outside. I saw Latch and Picket, and realized you were still in there."

Sadie's chest tightened. "I was okay," she said, her voice choked with tears. They were both okay. Much worse could have happened to them. They would survive this, and in a week, they'd be sitting together on this deck, drinking hot cocoa with peppermint schnapps and toasting to surviving.

"I'm quitting," Paige said. Her voice was still small.

"Don't you fucking dare," Sadie ground out.

"It's not worth all this."

Sadie took a deep breath. No two-timing sleazeball asshole billionaire was going to scare her friend away from her dreams.

"Jeannette Rankin."

"Jo Cox." Paige countered.

"Gabby Giffords."

"Damn you, Mastermind."

"Cori Bush. Nancy Fucking Pelosi."

"Okay."

"Shirley. Chisholm."

"I got it, Mastermind. I got it. You win."

"You win. Don't quit on me, Fence."

"Never." Paige's voice was strong and choked with tears. Just like hers. "Talk tomorrow?"

"Twenty-hundred. It's a date. Stay strong. Mastermind out."

Sadie tipped her head back and looked at the sky. The

clouds were low, reflecting the light of the town back on itself. She could see even the darkest corners of her yard. Snow was definitely coming. She couldn't believe that had worked. And Barry no longer owed her one, which was annoying because she'd kept that favor in her back pocket for years. Tinsley was turning six this year. Either way, worth it.

But what had she learned?

Paige didn't have a deep dark secret. Or even a Jackson-specific secret that could turn people off you in a second. She didn't ski in jeans. She didn't have an Ikon ski pass. She didn't travel over Teton Pass without snow tires when snow tires were required. She'd never, ever touched the stuffed bison on town square, and she hardly ever complained about the archaic post office. Truly, a model citizen.

So, Wade Fisher had resorted to what all weak men did—physical violence and threats. It made her blood boil. If he'd left so much as a bruise...which he probably had if he'd grabbed her. Mateo was smart. He would make sure those were photographed, would make sure the physical violence was considered.

But would that mean they would think she had killed him in self-defense?

With her...tampon? Sadie couldn't help but snicker.

Elijah Stanton was wrong. There was no killer oppo on Paige. In fact, there *was* killer opposition on Wade. He had a whole almost-teenager mistress. How had he kept her a secret?

* * *

The door opened behind her while she ruminated.

"The old pizza with a message in it trick," Merritt said, sinking into the seat beside her.

"You know that one?"

He smirked. "Used it at least once. Did you spell it out in olives?"

"Paige hates olives. No, I had Barry write it in Sharpie on the box under the pizza."

"Non-edible, though. You left evidence."

Sadie shrugged. "It's chilly tonight. Good night for a fire."

"You always were a mastermind," he chuckled. There was silence between them for a minute. "You know, if they were listening...they understood everything you said. Code names aren't supposed to be cute."

"Yeah," Sadie said. "I have to hope they're busy enough they're not listening. But I don't think anything I heard was something they haven't. Also, remind me to tell you about Agent Cooke tomorrow. She's...something else."

"Tomorrow? Why not now?"

Sadie yawned hugely. "I'm exhausted. And tomorrow I have to give a statement to said Agent and get a cast. I'll barely have time for investigating. Or forgiving you."

"But that's on the list?" He raised a hand, ghosting it over her ponytail. Just the barest hint of a touch. Her neck prickled, her skin wanting to be caressed. But he dropped his hand, smiling at her crookedly.

She looked back at him, solemnly. "Yeah. I'm sure it is. *As friends.*"

He nodded. "Of course."

"I'm not sure I'm up for anything more." Her body screamed at her she was lying. But the past year had taught her not to get too close. Not again.

He shrugged. "Well, I'm here. I'm not going anywhere. So..."

"In case I change my mind?"

He winked.

"Where are you living, anyway? And did you quit your job? Early retire? Or are you like…working remotely or something?"

"All questions I can answer another day," he promised. "For now, you need to go to bed." He tipped his head at the house, which had started thumping with bass. "I'll clear out the rowdy crew so you can rest."

"Thanks, Merritt," she said. Her eyes drooped. "I'll hate you less tomorrow."

"Promise?"

"Promise."

Chapter Sixteen

Getting a cast wasn't as fun as Sadie had imagined when Brooke Vassar broke her arm in fifth grade and came to school with a Barbie-pink cast everyone begged to autograph. In fact, it was uncomfortable, kind of stinky, and a little depressing. Because when you were thirty-three years old, they didn't ask you if you wanted a Barbie-pink cast. They presumed you wanted white. And Sadie had too much on her mind to correct them.

So, with a brand new, blazing white cast in her sling, she walked out into a new world.

Snow. As she'd predicted.

And maybe it was that shock to the system, going into the doctor's office with it cloudy, but the ground uncovered, and then coming out to everything covered in white, to barely being able to see her mom's car where they'd parked it, that made her remember the two things she'd forgotten.

The bomb.

And the blood.

Her mom could tell she was thinking hard. In the car, carefully negotiating the slick roads, she finally asked her. "What are you thinking about? Spill it. This is like when you'd be silent in the car on the drive home from school or practice and you'd be working up the courage to ask if Paige could sleep over on a school night."

"Which you always allowed."

"Because Paige's mom deserved a break," Robin shrugged. "And you two were less trouble together than apart."

"I forgot about the bomb," Sadie admitted. "I haven't been thinking about it at all."

"Well, like you asked at the press conference—"

Sadie blanched, not realizing her mom had witnessed *that* particular misadventure.

"—it could be two separate crimes."

"Right. And if they think it was Paige, then it had to be two crimes, right? How could she call in a bomb threat at the same time she was evacuating?" When she said it out loud, she realized that didn't work. Paige wasn't where she was supposed to be when she was evacuating, so she could've made a call.

But her call logs would show she hadn't. And so, the investigators would know she hadn't done it.

Paige probably wasn't a suspect in the bombing. So, who was?

"Who would want to disrupt the polling place?" Robin asked. "And just one? There are five polling places in Teton County, and they only targeted that one."

"Presuming it wasn't accidental."

"I think the presence of ATF and the fact a bomb threat was sent in indicates that," Robin said dryly.

True. Sadie's brain was trying to point something out to her, if only she could think hard enough. "If it was two crimes, then..." It finally came to her. "The killer didn't plan! It was a crime of opportunity. Which makes sense they used something they found on the scene to kill him."

"Nice deduction, Sherlock," Robin said, only a little sarcastic.

"Which brings us to the next thing I forgot."

"What's that?"

"The blood."

Robin blanched. She'd always been squeamish. Once, when Sadie had cut herself shaving as a teen, Robin had passed out while helping her bandage her ankle. "Yuck. Okay, pick another sidekick to deduce that with. I don't want to talk about blood." She pulled into a parking space in front of the bakery. "You sure you're okay here today? Wouldn't you rather go home and rest? The doctor said to rest."

Sadie shrugged. "I can rest in my office as well as the house, and I have work to get done. Though I'm not sure how good I'll be at spreadsheets with one hand."

"Make your dad do the spreadsheets," Robin suggested. "Or one of your business partners." She got out of the car and came around to help Sadie out. "Don't fall out here, it's slick."

"Thanks, mom." They walked up the shoveled steps to the bakery together. They stood under the awning, watching the snow come down, in silent companionship for a moment. "I'm sorry, by the way. Y'all probably wish you had already left for Arizona."

"Nope," Robin said. "We lived here long enough we can handle a little snow. We want to make sure you're okay before we leave."

Sadie couldn't help but feel guilty. She was a grown woman. Her parents shouldn't have to look after her. And it felt like it was happening too often, all because of these predicaments she kept getting involved in.

"Speaking of making sure you're okay..." Robin said slyly. "Tell me about Merritt being back in your life."

Sadie rolled her eyes. "He's been back in my life about

twelve hours, and I've only promised to hate him a little less today than I did yesterday. And he sent a text earlier that he's out of pocket all day because of unspecified business, which means he's still on his old bullshit."

Robin's lips twitched. "You couldn't hate that man, no matter what he did. Or what he does."

"I don't care if Ryan killed his entire family, he's like a son to me," Sadie giggled, quoting Michael from *The Office* talking about his favorite intern, Ryan.

Robin laughed. "Exactly. I'm thrilled to think you and Merritt might work things out."

"That's taking it way too fast, Mom. I'm not sure I'm up for anything else with him. And now is not the time."

"My girls!" Arlo came through the front door, eyes dancing. "It's snowing! The first snow of the year!" He was gleeful. He turned his eye to Snow King, the in-town resort that dominated the southern sky. "I bet we can get turns in this weekend."

Robin patted his arm. "We can stay at least that long, husband." While Arlo's sport of choice was skiing, Robin's was golfing. Sadie was confident they'd figure out the balance between her need for warmth and eternal sunshine and his need for snow. Eventually.

"Now I'm off," Robin said. "Book club's meeting at the library at nine, and I have *words* to say about the book they picked." She pecked Arlo on the cheek, then did the same to Sadie. "Promise you'll be good?"

"Promise, mom," Sadie said. Her and Arlo watched her cross the slick street to her car.

"Promise you'll be bad?" Arlo said in a villainous voice, and Sadie grinned. "Of course, Dad. Now, I need to talk to someone about blood splatter, and I can only imagine you're the one."

* * *

It was a little morbid, pretending to kill someone with a pen, but Arlo, a theater veteran, insisted on recreating the visual.

"Yes, wonderful," he said, watching Sage's controlled hand swing, pen gripped firmly, toward Kendall's neck. "Feel the movement, the moment," he coached.

Of course, Kendall had agreed to be the victim.

The pen gently tapped against Kendall's thorax, and she fell to the ground dramatically, tossing red sprinkles in the air to simulate blood.

"This is the strangest place I've ever worked," Max said, watching the spectacle. "And I was at a prison work camp for a year." Max had gotten into some trouble in their late teens and had completely turned their life around since.

Sadie looked at them sympathetically. "All that work to become an upstanding member of society, and you end up with us for company. My sympathies, friend."

"You're going to scare away the customers, *locos*," Jorge Garcia, Sadie's front of house manager, protested. He stood at the passthrough in the dining room, glowering into the kitchen. A big, broad Hispanic man, he'd retired from teaching high school and coaching the football team and worked the front while his grandkids were in preschool.

"If anything, we're giving them a bonus to their pastries," Kendall said from the floor. The red sprinkles scattered over her white t-shirt made Sadie's skin crawl. Maybe this was too much. She *had* just found a body two days ago. "A scone and a show!"

Arlo stood from where he'd been kneeling next to her. "Yeah, there's no way you could stab someone in the neck and not be covered with blood. Also, I looked it up on my phone, and it said it would be a bloody way to kill someone."

"Cool," Kendall said. "Can I get up now? I think I'm sitting in some lemon curd."

"Please," Sadie said. "I think we've had enough fun with this today. This is serious."

Max patted her shoulder. "It is. You're doing a good job. Did their demonstration help you at least?"

Sadie thought it through. "Yes? Paige wasn't covered in blood, so it couldn't have been her, right? But I didn't see *anyone* covered in blood, so what does that mean?"

"Maybe someone changed their clothes quickly?" Kendall said. She'd climbed off the floor and was dabbing lemon curd off her shoulder.

"And put them where?" They'd have been found in a trash can or nearby.

"The fire?" Jorge asked. "The building was on fire, *mija.*" He was being gentle with her, which meant he thought she was being an idiot.

That was a possibility, she supposed. But there hadn't been a lot of flame, even when Sadie left the building. And yes, she'd seen the fire damage to the building, so there had been flame, but not in the main exhibit hall. It'd all been out in the vestibule. Could the killer have thrown their bloody clothes into the fire, then exited? There would have been no guarantee the fire would eradicate the evidence, plus wouldn't that mean someone was outside without a coat on? That would've been obvious.

Sadie tried to think about what she'd seen when she'd come out. She'd been in pain and terrified. She hadn't been thinking clearly. But there was one person that had already been outside. Someone she needed to talk to, anyway, to confirm Elijah's story.

"Kendall?"

"Yes, boss?" She was inspecting the floor now. "Where did that lemon curd even come from?" She seemed bewildered. She looked up. "Oh. There it is."

"Sorry about that," Sage said, floating over to watch the drip of lemon curd. "Had a piping accident earlier, must have missed a spot."

"Well, one mystery solved," Kendall said, patting Sage's shoulder.

"Kendall."

She finally turned to Sadie with her full attention.

"Where's your fiancé?"

* * *

The answer was at work, which meant she was down the street at the recently opened Basecamp Cowork. Claire used to work out of her condo at the big resort, or occasionally a purloined conference room from the business suite offered to owners, but she'd recently started working there instead, to be closer to Kendall during the day.

It was so sweet it made Sadie's teeth hurt.

Kendall came along, so her and Sadie walked over together, snow falling gently on their heads. Only an inch or two had accumulated, and it seemed to be tapering off. Sadie's phone buzzed in her pocket, and she pulled it out. A text from Nora.

> They'd like you to come in today at 1PM to give your statement. Meet me there? Or I can give you a ride! Let me know!

Sadie was glad she didn't have to dislike Nora anymore, because she was almost impossible to dislike. She tapped out a quick reply, letting her know she'd meet her at the police station, and then refocused on her walk with Kendall.

"Make any wedding plans recently?" Sadie asked. The two had gotten engaged over Valentine's Day and had frenetically made wedding plans until Kendall's ADHD hyperfocus had lasered somewhere else.

Kendall smiled. "Not yet. I think Claire wants to formally set a date, but I'm enjoying being engaged."

"There's no rush," Sadie assured her. "As long as you make sure we have enough time to make the cake."

Kendall's eyes turned dreamy. "Oh, I've thought about the cake. That reminds me. Construction's going great out in Wilson. I checked in yesterday."

"I need to swing by, too," Sadie sighed. "I haven't been in a week or so. Have they got the kitchen in yet?"

"Almost."

"Exciting." When Sadie had opened her first coffee kiosk south of Jackson in the commuting hub of Hoback Junction, she'd dreamed of opening more, but knew she needed time to get the financing. Then Claire swooped in, and she offered way better interest rates than banks. The three of them had formally entered a business partnership for the coffee kiosks, and now had three open with a fourth opening after the first of the year. Every commuter into Jackson would be well-caffeinated and fed, and it made Sadie's heart sing to think about it. As part of the partnership, Claire had also purchased an old office building located twenty minutes west of Jackson and they were converting it into a commercial kitchen to supply the kiosks, as well as do their specialty bakes. As a bonus, the top floor was being converted into employee housing. It was Sadie's proudest business accomplishment, and she was thrilled to be in business with her friends.

"Have you...thought about hiring?"

Sadie pulled a face. "No. Although I have a lead on a baker that's working at the Whole Grocer...I need to scope them out and see if we can recruit them. I've heard she does great cakes."

"And if we're getting in the wedding cake business, we'll need her," Kendall confirmed. They paused in front of the cowork space, and Sadie blew out a breath.

"The last time I was in this building, I was snooping around to figure out who killed Sloan Brackendridge," Sadie admitted.

"Scenic View Realty and Property Management is no more," Kendall said. She bumped Sadie's good shoulder and winked. "May it burn in hell."

Chapter Seventeen

The cowork space had kept the bones of Scenic View but had lightened and brightened up the space. Where Scenic View had been cold, all granite and glass, Basecamp Cowork was light wood with copious amounts of plants. The inner bullpen was an open workspace, where creatives and entrepreneurs worked at long tables, some chatting, some focused. Around the outside, where the realtor offices had been, were the private suites they rented out. In the back corner was Claire's office.

She was on a call when they tapped on her door, but she hung up quickly, getting up to open the door to them. She looked at Sadie with concern. "Trippy being here?"

"Beyond," Sadie laughed.

"Same, honestly," Claire said. "But this is a place of creation, not destruction. It feels good, the way it's changed. Now. I imagine you're here to ask me more questions?"

Sadie nodded.

"Come in and settle, then, Detective Holmes."

"What am I, day old bagels?" Kendall groused.

"Of course, come along Dr. Watson," Claire said, rolling her eyes. The two bantered for a minute while Sadie sat, propping her arm on a throw pillow. Her arm felt better in the cast. More stable. But it was already itching.

"On Election Day, did you see Elijah Stanton outside?" Sadie asked when she had Claire's attention.

Claire pursed her lips, thinking. "Yes...I did. He came out shortly after me, actually. He went around the side of the building, talking on his phone, but yeah, he was outside too. Let me guess. He's not registered here, either?"

Kendall frowned at Claire. "We have to fix that. You live here now, babe."

"I know," Claire said, patting Kendall's knee. "It's business reasons I'm still a Chicagoan."

"Did you notice anyone without a coat, or jacket, once they'd evacuated?" Sadie asked.

Claire cocked her head. "Yeah, actually. Paige and Luna didn't have their coats."

Sadie blinked. "What?"

"Yeah, that's one of the reasons I thought it was best they get in their car and go home, because Luna was cold."

Sadie swallowed hard. Did that mean something? She'd convinced herself that whoever didn't have a coat was the killer, but...Paige didn't have a coat. She thought back. Paige and Luna had been wearing their matching pantsuits. And Kamari had thought they were cute. Which means...right. She remembered, now. Paige had taken off her and Luna's coats so they'd match. And she'd tucked them under her arm. When they were in line in front of her, waiting to go into the booths, Paige and Mateo had been holding ballots, but their arms had been full. Mateo's full of Luna, and Paige's full of coats.

"Okay. I remember them taking their coats off. It makes sense they'd lose them in the chaos. But did you notice anyone else?" This was a good theory, and she wanted it to prove correct.

"I didn't, but now that I'm thinking of it...I did take a couple pictures."

"What?" Sadie was shocked. "That would have been super helpful to know!"

"I forgot," Claire shrugged. "We've kind of been through a lot in the last couple days, you know?" She scrolled through her phone, then looked at Sadie. "I airdropped them to you."

Sadie accepted the drop, then pulled them up. "Wow."

"Yeah, it was a lot of smoke. Like, a lot a lot."

She zoomed in on the first photo. From Claire's position in front of the building, she'd captured a great wide shot, but the people weren't the focus. She checked the timestamps. The first had been taken at 9:56 A.M., two minutes after Kamari first saw the smoke, and it was billowing out of the building's vestibule. The next few were at 9:58 A.M., with a large crowd gathered outside. Most everyone had been evacuated at that point. It was such a brief window! How had so many things gone wrong in such a short amount of time? Thinking back on it, it seemed like it had taken Sadie hours to slog through the smoke toward the door, looking for Paige. But it had to have been less than three minutes. And in that time? Someone had murdered Wade Fisher.

Sadie zoomed in on the crowd. She spotted Elijah Stanton, standing off alone. He wasn't wearing a coat. Was that suspicious? But he'd been outside the whole time, right? She studied his form. He was wearing a thick, outdoorsy fleece. Maybe he was just warm blooded.

She looked for Madison Fisher, but she didn't see her. Sadie thought about where she'd been when she came out the door and realized she was probably looking at a bad angle.

She scrolled forward. One more picture. This one had flame

licking out the roof of the building. The smoke was black, oily. Sadie shuddered. In this photo, Claire had moved toward the side of the building Sadie had come out of. In fact...that was her. Coming out as the firefighter came in. Sadie groaned. "Uh, you got a picture of *me*," she complained.

Kendall pulled the phone closer to study it. "You look like some sort of Valkyrie returning from war. You're sooty and injured, but you look ready to kill someone."

Sadie chuckled. "That's my terrified face, not my about to kill someone face. I'd just found a dead body."

Kendall shrugged, handing the phone back to her. "Same same."

Sadie scanned the photo again, remembering where Madison had been. And there she was, at the front of the crowd. Sadie could see her blonde hair, the arm crooked up, holding her phone to her ear. She imagined her the way she'd seen her when she'd stumbled out of the building. Eyes wide, sobbing, pleading into her phone for her husband to pick up. The sun had glinted off the diamonds she wore on her fingers. And she'd been wearing...a Fisher for Mayor shirt.

Sadie stood up, heart beating fast. Yes! When she'd first seen her that morning, she'd been wearing a coat zipped to her chin. Gretchen said she'd warned her she couldn't wear a political t-shirt at the polling place, so Madison had zipped her coat up. And then, a few minutes later, she hadn't had a coat on. This was it!

"What, boss?" Kendall asked excitedly.

Sadie held the phone out to her. "Is Madison Fisher wearing a coat in this picture?"

Kendall squinted at it, zooming it in, then out, then in again.

"Yes."

Sadie's shoulders drooped. "What?"

"Yeah, you can see here, where her arm is crooked? That's her red coat. No one else nearby is wearing red."

Shit.

"Well, there goes that theory," Sadie sighed, sinking back down into her chair. "I thought I had it, but she'd unzipped it. Probably for the publicity. Shoot." She scanned the photos again. "Thanks for these, anyway," Sadie said. "I don't see anyone out of place, though. No one who looks like they've just stabbed someone."

"And yet, someone did," Claire said. "Tell me what you've figured out so far."

Sadie thought about it.

"Well. Considering the improvised tool of death, I feel like it was a crime of opportunity, not pre-planned."

"So, the bomb was separate?"

"I think so. The timing is so bad. And the police will figure out who called in the bomb threat. I don't know how you'd even do that these days without getting caught."

"True."

"Someone in that building killed him. And it wasn't me. Or Paige. When I left my booth, I saw Mateo with Luna, and Paige wasn't with him. Now I know Wade had grabbed Paige and pulled her aside, threatening her with violence to quit the race."

Kendall tensed. "Seriously?"

"Yep."

"I mean. I'd kill him again if he wasn't already dead," Kendall said, tightening her fists. "How dare he."

"Same. That's why we didn't see her. I told Mateo to leave out the closest door, and I turned to go out the other door, looking for Paige as I went. Paige said she struggled, and that must be when she dropped the pen. She got away and ran out the door."

"Wait, wait, wait," Kendall said. "I can't do this auditory-only thing. Draw me a picture. Where was everyone? Where were the doors?"

That was a good idea. Claire handed Sadie a notebook and pen, and she drew it out. She marked the doors, and the voting booths everyone had gone into, as far as she remembered. S for her, P for Paige, M for Mateo, and W for Wade. She wasn't sure where Madison had been. An X marked the spot she'd tripped over Wade.

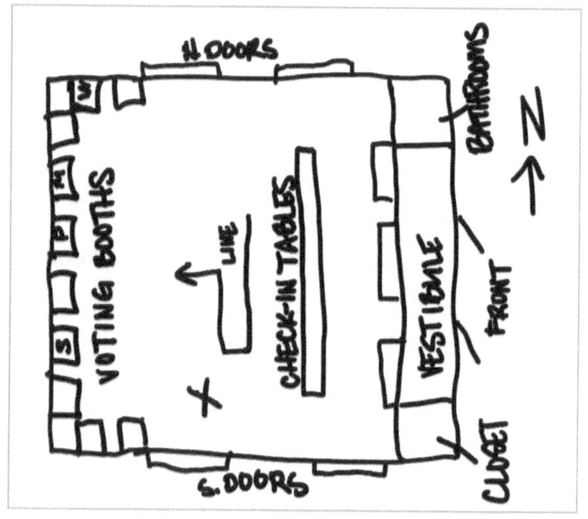

"Okay," Kendall said. "Now I see. So, you eventually went out the south door, but Mateo and Luna left out the north door."

"Yes."

"And it didn't really matter in the end, because they herded everyone around to the front of the building, more toward the south door, as the firefighters arrived," Claire said. "That's why in that last photo, I'm closer to that side of the building."

"Did you see Paige come out?" Sadie asked.

"I didn't," Claire frowned. "She came around the side of the building as we were being herded. She reunited with Mateo and realized you were still inside. The firefighters had just gotten there, so they wouldn't let her go back in. She caused a bit of a kerfuffle, actually."

"Enough that someone could've come out the south door without being noticed?" Sadie asked.

"Maybe. But there were dozens of people there, it was a chaotic scene."

Kendall was still studying the diagram. "I can see how it happened. Paige and Mateo leave their booths next to each other, but Wade is over along the side here," she gestured at the diagram. "He grabs Paige and pulls her to the side. Mateo doesn't notice for a few steps, and by then they're disguised by smoke, or behind the voting booths. That's when you see Mateo, Sadie."

"And I go the other direction, and he goes out the door. Paige struggles, gets away, and runs toward the door. I heard...I heard footsteps at one point. A shout, and footsteps. I wonder if that was her? I'd thought it was the murderer...but then I stumbled across the body. How did that happen?"

"Someone was watching," Claire said quietly. "They saw the altercation. They saw the pen...and they took the chance."

There was a shout nearby, and Kendall jumped up, frowning. "Something's going on," she said, rushing out of the office.

Sadie and Claire followed. They could hear sirens, and a red ladder truck went flying by, headed east. Then a police car, and another fire truck. They stepped out onto the sidewalk, gawking.

Then Sadie saw the plume of smoke. It was a few blocks away. Past town square.

Right about where Moose's was.

* * *

This couldn't be happening.

Not Moose's. Not her parent's legacy they'd entrusted to her, that she'd been making her own for the last eight years. Not Moose's.

As they drew closer, moving as quickly as they could with the slick sidewalks and the crowds on the streets watching the law enforcement, ambulance, and fire vehicles stack up, Sadie changed her mantra. Moose's was her legacy, but it was also her family. The building could go up in flames, as long as everyone was okay. *Please let everyone be okay*, she begged.

She saw Max first. They towered above everyone else, and her legs almost went out from under her she was so excited to see them. She pushed her way through the crowd, her casted arm aching from jostling it, and almost fell to her knees to sob. Everyone was gathered outside. Arlo had his arm around Sage, who was leaning on Max. Jorge was patting Arlo's shoulder. They all watched the building.

With grim resolve, Sadie turned her focus to it. And breathed a huge sigh of relief.

It appeared to be okay.

White smoke billowed up from behind the bakery, but she didn't see any flame, any dark, oily smoke of wood burning.

"Dad!" She said, skidding to a stop next to them. "What happened! Is everyone okay?"

Arlo pulled her close, wrapping her up tight. "Everyone's okay, sugar bug," he promised. "Everyone got out."

"We smelled smoke in the back," Max said, their voice brittle. "We checked all the machinery, checked the ovens. Nothing was smoking. Then smoke started coming in under the back door, so we called 911."

"Thank goodness you're all okay," Sadie cried, hugging Sage, then Max, then Jorge. Kendall and Claire followed, all of them clutching each other.

"The smoke's dying down," Arlo said, a hopeful note in his voice. "Maybe it's okay."

Sadie grasped his hand. "Moose's is fine. Because we're Moose's."

He looked at her, teary. "You're right. You're always right."

"But one can hope," Claire said from beside him. "Terrible amount of paperwork, casualty insurance."

After the smoke dissipated, things started happened pretty quickly.

The ambulances left empty, a few fire trucks pulled away.

But the ATF van arrived.

And that's when Sadie realized. This wasn't some bizarre coincidence, being involved in two fires in as many days. This was connected. And someone had just come after her.

Chapter Eighteen

They were allowed into the bakery after half an hour of waiting in the cold, snow gathering on their coats. A windbreaker-wearing Black man with a buzz cut and dark sunglasses who did not introduce himself watched them from the doorway. Sadie checked their exterior cameras, but found the snow had covered them, rendering them useless. So much for technology.

"Someone needs to invent little bitty windshield wipers for cameras," Kendall mused.

Maybe the businesses behind them in the alley had footage the police could use to identify how the fire had started, but Sadie didn't.

Sadie texted Nora, and she jetted over to wait with them, introducing herself to everyone and becoming one of them within minutes. Sadie knew she'd also have to call her insurance agent, Sandeep, and her corporate lawyers, too. But for now, this was enough. Because whatever had happened, it was connected to Wade's murder. She was sure of it. Maybe she'd been too hasty to decide the crimes were unconnected. She shouldn't have discounted that someone could've worked with a partner. One person to call in the bomb, another to murder Wade.

But who?

Her suspects were so slim. Elijah and Madison? That was it? And neither of them seemed to have a motive. If Wade divorced Madison like he'd promised Ashleigh, Sadie was sure Madison would still get a bunch of money. And Madison had seemed very ready for the First Lady of Jackson role, having shown up to many events during the campaign dressed like the President of the Women's League. And Elijah and Wade were friends. Genuine friends, the kind that recognized each other's faults and foibles. He knew Wade wasn't the best kind of man, and he helped him anyway. Why would he kill him? And he'd been outside the polling place during the murder. He couldn't have gone in through a side door, they were locked from the outside.

Unless someone let him in? But when would they have had time?

Sadie couldn't help but feel like she'd missed something huge. But the killer hadn't. They'd noticed her asking questions, sniffing around the suspects the investigators were ignoring while they focused in on Paige. And who had she questioned?

Elijah. Madison. Ashleigh.

Ashleigh. Did her flighty, materialistic exterior hide a cagey genius? Eh. That seemed like taking it a little too far. And why would she kill him? With him dead, she'd fully admitted her lifestyle was going to change.

Agent Cooke entered, and she lost her train of thought.

"Ms. Moose," she said, coming in and looking around. "I had a scone you made yesterday. It was fantastic."

"It wasn't made by me," Sadie said, gesturing at her staff. "They're the amazing ones. And please call me Sadie."

"Sadie. Can I talk to you...alone?" She looked at the gathered crowd with suspicion.

"Please, go ahead, Alice," Sadie encouraged. "This one is my lawyer." Nora waved happily. "And the rest? Trust me, they'll all know within five minutes, anyway. What's going on?"

Agent Cooke looked skeptical but continued, anyway. "As you've probably noticed, there is no damage to the interior of the building. You'll want to get your own insurance inspectors in here, but the device that set off the smoke was in the back dumpster. It didn't ignite anything, so this was just a smoke show."

What Sadie heard that Agent Cooke hadn't said was that it didn't ignite anything *this time*.

"Of course, the quick thinking by your staff helped," she said. "It's possible without being rapidly attended to, the situation could've been worse."

"Well, they all deserve at least a pizza party," Sadie said, trying for funny despite the tears clogging her voice. Max patted her shoulder.

"Is this connected to the polling place smoke bomb?" Arlo asked, and Sadie looked at him in surprise. She wasn't the only one. Agent Cooke looked at him warily. "Oh please," he sighed. "I've hung around enough stages to recognize theatrical smoke. Let me guess. An Enola Gaye? Those things produce so much smoke. Remote detonation is possible, too. Which is handy for a criminal that wants to not be seen at the venue."

There was dead silence in the room.

"Arlo Moose, everyone," Kendall said, beginning a slow clap that quickly sped up as everyone joined in. He gave a little bow, and Agent Cooke let out a bark of laughter.

"Okay, I can neither confirm nor deny anything you said, but I will say...keen mind on that one."

"He's my dad," Sadie said proudly, and Agent Cooke looked delighted.

"Sleuthing runs in the family?" Arlo tipped an invisible hat, and she chucked. "Well, I can confirm we're investigating a connection," she conceded. "Which I'm sure you deduced from the ATF response. And this dude." She nodded at the windbreaker-wearing agent, who tipped his head at her respectfully. "Now, I'd like to ask some questions if that's okay? I'm afraid it will be a grueling process, but I'm glad your legal representation is here."

"Happy to help, everyone!" Nora chirped. "Do you mind if I record? Of course, Wyoming being a one-party state, I don't have to ask but I like to be polite when I can."

"Totally fine with me," Agent Cooke said.

She wasn't lying that it was grueling. With the help of two assistants she brought in, they questioned everyone. Where had they been when they noticed the smoke? Where had they been on Election Day? They were trying to connect anything and anyone. But Sadie knew they were all innocent, and Nora was there to watch over them, and it all went okay in the end. When they'd finished, Agent Cooke had a clearer picture of Election Day. She'd gotten Claire's photos, which she'd been very pleased with, and Sadie's official statement, too.

"Honestly, this was pretty convenient," Agent Cooke admitted at the end of the marathon when she pulled Sadie aside.

"Less for us," Sadie sighed. "We have to throw out a lot of goods. Just in case. And we lost half a day's business. And probably tomorrow, too. I have a mountain of work to do."

"Then I'll get out of your hair. Which is different today? Anything new you'd like to share with me?"

"Oh, yesterday I was in disguise," Sadie admitted. She

thought over what she'd learned. "Do you know about... uh...Ashleigh?"

"Yes," Agent Cooke said immediately. "She's something else. Not a suspect, as far as we can tell. Airtight alibi for yesterday morning."

"Where was she?"

"In the salon chair at Bad Hair Day."

"Ah," Sadie sighed. "Okay. I didn't think she had anything to do with it." But Sadie might call her friend, Juliana, who worked at the salon. Just to dish.

"Then no," Sadie admitted. "I'm stymied. There doesn't seem to be a good motive to have him dead. Unless...I'm sure y'all have checked the will and stuff?"

"It's not quite that easy," Agent Cooke said, "but yeah, we're looking into it." Her phone buzzed, and she pulled it out of its holster to look at the screen. "Excuse me," she said, stepping outside.

"So, are we clear to clean?" Max asked.

"We need pictures. At least. I'm surprised Sandeep hasn't busted down our door yet."

"I'll call him," Arlo said. "I'm not on the policy anymore but I'm his youngest's godfather. If he can't come over, he'll tell us what to do."

Sadie thanked him, but then she caught a view of Agent Cooke outside. She was standing ramrod straight, and her eyes were boring into hers. With robotic precision, she pulled the phone away from her ear. Her eyes wide and sad, she mouthed two words at Sadie, then turned and ran for her car.

Sadie's heart pounded.

"I'm sorry."

She'd said, "I'm sorry."

Paige.

* * *

Sadie made Kendall drive her, and they arrived at Paige's house moments after Agent Cooke did. Just in time to see Paige being led from her house, her hands handcuffed behind her back. Her eyes were red but tear-free, her head held high. The news crews that filmed greedily from the sidewalk captured her defiant walk. Later, in news stories, they'd call it proud. Like that was a bad thing.

Sadie didn't see Mateo. She assumed he was inside with Luna, and the thought made her eyes water. That poor baby. She needed her mama.

What evidence had the police found that made the arrest possible? Whatever it was, they'd acted on it quickly.

Like Penny was reading her mind, her phone dinged with a text message from her.

> Bad news. Arresting Paige. Source says they found burned fragments of Paige's coat with blood splatter on it. DNA still pending but seems pretty cut and dry. Still know she didn't do it.

Her coat. Her damn coat. Sadie had known it was missing, she'd figured that out this morning. But now it was being used against her. How had blood gotten on it? Had it been near Wade's body? Sadie scraped her memory from that terrible morning, but she hadn't seen Paige's camel-colored coat nearby.

She showed the text to Kendall.

"Damn, damn, damn," Kendall said from the driver's seat. "Damn! How? This is such a setup. This sucks. Majorly. Poor Mateo and Luna."

"And I have nothing," Sadie said through tears. "I have no

other viable suspects to offer. I've failed her. And I've failed Mateo, and I've failed my little godbaby."

Kendall leaned over, wrapping her arms around her awkwardly. "You haven't failed, sis. You're just in the dark night of the soul."

Sadie snorted, tears still falling. "This isn't the hero's journey, Kendall. It's the hero's downfall. I don't even know what to do next."

"Pssshhh," Kendall scoffed. "I do."

"You do?"

Kendall handed her a packet of tissues from her center console. "Yep. You sit back and dry your eyes and let me lead for a bit."

She put on a pair of mirrored aviator sunglasses, then turned to Sadie, the reflection blinding her. "It's go time," she said, her voice low.

"Eh," Sadie sniffed.

"You're right, you're right. Let me think." Kendall took off her sunglasses, pinching the bridge of her nose. "Aha! Okay, prepare yourself."

Sadie shook off the tears. "Okay. Okay, I'm ready."

Kendall looked up slowly, then slipped on the sunglasses, turning toward an imaginary camera behind Sadie. "This ballot box...was stuffed with malice."

It made no sense, and that was enough to make Sadie laugh. Kendall grinned at her. "Okay, let's go. I really do know what to do next."

* * *

"Kendall, I can't even drink. How is getting drunk at a dive bar in the middle of the afternoon on a Thursday going to help anything?" Sadie frowned up at the building in front of her. It was on the outskirts of South Jackson, a large, multi-story wood building with no name that advertised "beer in the back." She gestured at her arm. "And I can't even drive you home if you get wasted."

"Dude, my fiancé has a driver. It's cool. Sully loves this place. Last summer we were here, and he pool sharked a guy out of so much money. He took a cue to the face. It almost straightened out his nose once and for all. Then Bax sat on the guy, and Sully bought the bar a round with the money and we were all good. We're all friends on BeReal now."

"Wait, I remember that TikTok. Didn't that get you a sponsorship deal with a pool cue company?"

"Righteous, it totally did. Paid off the last of the student loans with those deliverables. Who knew, right? It's a brave new world."

"Who drove you home that night?"

"Claire Bear," Kendall sighed. "We were all in the doghouse a while. Anyway, this isn't just any dive bar." She brandished her arms in a magician's flourish. "This is the dive bar where Wade Fisher's weirdo lawyer likes to hang out and get chatty."

Sadie gawked at her. "How on earth..."

"If I told you, you wouldn't think I was mysterious anymore, and it involves a lot of cousin's brother's wife's sister's kind of connections. Best just to take my info and follow my lead." Which Sadie did, because what were her other options? Sadie trudged around the side of the building behind Kendall, their footsteps muddy where the fresh snow had melted once the sky cleared, and the sun came out. Everything would be covered in ice in the morning if it didn't snow more.

To Sadie's surprise, the back of the building had a large wraparound deck overlooking the Rafter J neighborhood and Snake River as it wound its way through the valley. Most of the land they saw was under a conservation easement, though developers had floated different land swap ideas to build housing. They'd all been shot down, though, so for now, Sadie enjoyed the open space view. Kendall nudged her, and they entered through the back door.

It was raucous, even in the middle of the afternoon.

The high-ceilinged room was paneled in wood, neon beer and liquor signs lighting up the space. In the center was a large, rectangular bar with barstools all the way around it. More than half of them were filled. *Sportscenter* and various sportsball games flashed on the big screen TVs, and country music poured out of the jukebox. A half dozen patrons were at the aforementioned pool tables, but it looked like the game was friendly. It smelled like fried food and stale beer, but it was homey, not grimy.

"This isn't actually a dive bar," Sadie said to Kendall accusingly. She picked her feet up and down to demonstrate. "See? My feet don't even stick."

Kendall shrugged. "It's not, but the Coop likes to think of themselves as one. Now let's get a drink." She led the way to the bar and pushed herself onto a stool. Sadie followed. The bartender came over and him and Kendall executed a complicated handshake Sadie couldn't decipher. He was a white man in his late twenties with a non-ironic mustache and a permanent sunglasses tan. He gave her finger guns when Kendall introduced her as "the incomparable Sadie Moose, my boss—I mean business partner—and friend."

Sadie waved, unable to come up with a gesture as cool as finger guns on such short notice.

"Sadie, this is Jack, bartender extraordinaire and my favorite raft guide in the watershed."

"Nice to meet you, Jack. I'm sure you have stories about Kendall."

"She ever tell you about the time we dump trucked a bachelorette party, and I ended up married to the bride? That was my first annulment."

"If I didn't know a dump truck was when everyone in the raft was tossed out in a rapid, I'd be blushing," Sadie deadpanned, and Jack winked at her.

"What can I get ya?"

"She'll have a Dr. Pepper and an order of mozzarella sticks." Sadie beamed. That was her order. Her friend knew her so well! "And I'll have whatever your fave on tap is and a burger, please. And if you can point out Billy Pierce...?"

Jack's gaze sharpened as he poured a tall glass of creamy porter. He waggled his eyebrows, then nodded behind them. Sadie barely managed not to whip her head around. She looked into the mirror behind the bar instead, finding the frizzy-haired white man deep into a whiskey in a booth behind her.

"His drink's a Wyoming Whiskey neat, and he's two in," Jack said in a low voice as he put their drinks down in front of them. "And he enjoys the French Onion soup if you really want to butter him up."

"Then one of each, please," Sadie said. "I need him well buttered for what I need to ask him."

Chapter Nineteen

Once Kendall and Sadie had fortified their bodies with food—Sadie had bad news for Nash the next time she saw him, she had a new favorite mozzarella stick in town—and beverages, including a Dr. Pepper refill, they formulated their plan.

With a whiskey in one hand and soup in the other, Kendall approached, Sadie behind her. She'd said she'd take the reins, and she was doing so.

"Hey man," Kendall said, sliding the food and drink onto the table. "Heard you might've had a tough week."

Billy's eyes were red and glassy. Jack may have thought he was on his second whiskey, but Sadie could tell he was deeper than that. Like he hadn't stopped drinking in a few days. A little over forty-eight hours had passed since Wade's death. He might've been drinking for most of them. He studied them, eyes wavering from one to the other, then his hand reached for the whiskey, pulling it closer.

"And French Onion," Sadie said. "We heard it was your fave."

"Someone's been talkin'," Billy said, his voice slurred. "Thas okay. You brought food, thas okay. You wanna sit down? I could use someone to talk to."

"Sure," Kendall said, and the two of them slid into the booth across from him.

They introduced themselves, and Billy showed no recognition of either of them. He took a bite of the soup and bread though, which Sadie thought was a good sign.

Though if she was a good detective, she supposed she should want to get him drunker, so he'd answer more questions. But that didn't feel right. Billy was having a bad time, and she didn't like that for him.

"What's going on, Billy?" Sadie asked.

He slurped his soup. "You ever have to give someone bad news?"

"Yeah. It's no fun," Sadie commiserated.

"I had to tell my parents I was dropping out of school with over a 100K in student loans to move to Jackson to be a raft guide. I'm familiar."

Billy snorted. "Should've stuck it out for a degree."

Kendall snorted. "It worked out. And the world didn't need another lawyer."

Sadie looked at her in surprise. She'd never known that Kendall had been in law school. She bumped her with her shoulder. "You would've been a good one," she said.

"Meh."

"Better than me," Billy said, his voice thick. He took a slug of whiskey.

"Why?" Sadie asked.

"I worked for him," he muttered to himself. "She didn't know. It's not right."

Kendall threw her a glance. "You okay, Billy? Need us to call someone for you?"

"No one to call," he groused. "Gotta give bad news, then there really will be no one."

"Sometimes it helps to talk it through with someone else first," Sadie said. "Would that help you?"

Billy didn't answer, intent on slurping soup. He was about to hit the bottom. "Want another?" Kendall asked, but he didn't answer, polishing it off and shoving the bread in his mouth.

"He's dead, so I can talk," he mumbled into his whiskey.

Sadie gave Kendall a look. This didn't feel good. Kendall seemed to agree. "Man, can we get you a ride home?"

Billy looked up at them then, his gaze sharper than when they'd sat. The soup seemed to have sobered him up a bit. "Why do you care?"

Sadie waffled. Should she tell him?

He snorted. "I don't care why. I don't care anymore. I did it, and I'll stand by it." He took a deep breath. "I have to tell a widow she gets nothing," he slurred. "Nothing."

Sadie froze, her mind reeling. How could that be possible? Kendall put her hand on her thigh under the table, squeezing it. She wanted Sadie to let her handle this.

"That sounds unfair to me, bro," Kendall said.

"It is!" He raised his glass. "It is." He downed it morosely. "But I was doing my job." He sneered. "Just doing my job," he parroted. "And now that sweet woman...nothing."

Sadie had a hard time seeing Madison as sweet...but she was pretty sure that's who he was talking about.

"Why'd it go down that way?" Kendall asked, signaling to Jack to bring another round.

He waved them both to come closer, and they leaned in. He made them wait, then said on a potent whiskey breath, "secrets."

"Oh," Kendall said matter-of-factly. "Well, that makes sense."

"Secrets she didn't know," he said earnestly. "Other people he owes. So, they get it all, and she gets nothing."

"Should've gotten a prenup, I guess," Sadie mused.

Billy slammed his empty glass on the table, making her jump. He pointed a shaking finger at her. "That's jush it," he slurred. "She did. And in it, she knew she got nothing. That's the only way he'd get married. The bastard."

"Oh shit," Kendall breathed. "She gets nothing nothing. No settlement. Just...kicked out by his heirs?"

His head drooped. "I gotta tell her. Tomorrow. Why couldn't the bastard do it for me?"

Jack brought their round, and Billy took the glass greedily. "Should've heard her, when she found out he was dead," he said, sniffling. "Poor woman. Called me right away, so panicked. So upset."

Sadie reached across the table and patted his hand, and he looked up at her gratefully.

"You're both being very kind. I don't know why, but I thank you."

"What time is your meeting tomorrow?" Kendall asked.

Billy frowned at his watch. "Eight."

"Then that should probably be your last one, man. Can we give you a ride out of here when you're done with that? Or call you a cab? An Uber?"

He waved a hand. "I'm staying."

"You'll feel better if you're clearheaded tomorrow," Kendall insisted. "I know you don't want to do it. But do it for her. She needs you to be at the top of your game."

Billy thought about, and his shoulders drooped. "You're right," he croaked. "This is my last one."

Kendall signaled for water, and Sadie slumped back in the booth in relief. She wasn't supposed to kind of like Billy. But he sketched a tragic character, drinking himself silly because he had to tell a woman bad news.

"Could she contest it?" Sadie asked as he took his first sip of non-alcohol.

He pulled a face. "Long odds. Needs lots of money. Which she won't have."

"Did you know that the traditional gift for women has been jewelry throughout history not because we like shiny things, but because it was all women could accept as currency?" Kendall said, musing. "She must've collected her fair share of shiny things over the years. Maybe that's enough to contest it."

Billy squinted at her. "Aren't you a fella?"

Kendall shimmied. "Nope. Fair, though. I have short hair and I'm buff af."

"I don't know what that means," he slurred, rubbing his eyes. "I'm gettin tired."

"Then let's get you home," Sadie said.

* * *

That's how she ended up in the back of an SUV driven by a former NFL defensive linebacker squished between a sobering lawyer and an inebriated Kendall at five o'clock at night. The sun hadn't even set. Sadie was stone-cold sober, her arm aching, her head spinning. Meanwhile, Billy and Kendall were singing an epic rendition of Bon Jovi's *Livin' on a Prayer*. Sadie met Baxter's eyes in the mirror. He winked at her, and she winked back.

They dropped Billy off at his condo near Snow King. "Bye, Billy!" Kendall called. She held up her phone. "I'll call you! Let's do bingo night at the Elks next week!"

"You got it, K-dog!" Billy said, leaning on the SUV doorframe. "And thanks you two. Tomorrow is gonna suck, but I need to be sober. For her!"

"For her," Sadie agreed. He saluted them and stumbled to his door. Once he'd gone inside, Bax pulled away from the curb.

"Where to next, ladies?"

"Out!" Kendall called. "Let's go out!"

Sadie shook her head. "Home for me, please. You can take Ms. Rowdy anywhere you'd like, but I need a pain pill and a couch."

Bax pointed the SUV that way.

"Thanks, Kendall," Sadie said, reaching over to pat her arm. "I appreciate you taking the lead."

"What do you think it means?" Kendall asked.

"I've been thinking about it. It could be a motive. If Madison knew her prenup said she'd get nothing if he divorced her and didn't have a specific settlement for her on his death... then she could've thought she'd get the money as his wife in his will. Kill him before he could divorce her."

Kendall whistled. "Or do we need to think bigger? Who were the heirs? Did they do this? Get antsy for the money? Out of towners, I'm guessing? Could they have hired the whole thing out? Someone to set the bomb, someone to do the murder?"

"But the pen!" Sadie said. "They had about three minutes to commit the murder. When I found him, he was *dead*. Not gasping, not twitching. *Dead*."

"But no one could've planned to use the pen," Kendall argued. "Except Paige, and she didn't get it from Mateo until that morning. And we know she didn't do it. So, whoever the killer is, they chose in the moment to use the pen. It was spontaneous."

"Spontaneous method of death, but not necessarily unplanned. You're right."

Sadie sat back in her seat. "I still don't know. And I'm not sure what's next."

"I'm also running low on ideas," Kendall said, yawning. "Which is something for me. Man, I might not be up to party, actually. Maybe we should both curl up with a heating pad."

"But Paige," Sadie sighed. "She's *in jail*. She's my best friend, and she's in jail. In the town that she's on the town council for! She...ooh, have you checked the mayor results?"

Kendall blinked at her. "I managed to forget. It's consumed our lives for months...and I forgot."

Bax cleared his throat. "I didn't. She won. By over 1,200 votes. The results are unofficial, and I don't know if anyone would let her stand as mayor at this point, but she won."

"Of course she did. This is all such a waste," Sadie groaned. "We should be celebrating her, not trying to get her out of jail."

"C'mon, Moose. Listen. We'll figure this out. It's been a wild couple of days. There's nothing we can do to get Paige out tonight. So, let's all rest, and tomorrow we regroup. The bakery's closed. I'll get us a breakfast reservation. We'll hold a summit. A free-Paige, everything-on-the-table summit. And we'll figure it out."

Sadie thought about it. She could use a quiet evening. A quiet house. Of course, Gavin would eventually show to protect her from his guest bedroom, which seemed even more important considering what had happened at Moose's earlier.

"You're on," Sadie said. "Let's do it. Tomorrow, we figure this out. Together."

Chapter Twenty

Sadie's phone vibrating off her bedside table and thumping onto the carpeted floor awoke her at three in the morning.

She'd been dreaming, and it took her a moment to come out of it. But her phone persisted vibrating, and Tyrone, asleep at the end of her bed, grunted. He wanted her to make the noise go away, so he could go back to sleep. Lazy bones.

Then the haze of sleep lifted, and Sadie scrambled to grab her phone, jostling her arm. She cursed from the pain, but no one called at three in the morning if it wasn't an emergency.

She finally reached the phone, peering at it. An unknown number. Based on her complicated do not disturb settings, that meant they'd called at least twice already.

Hesitantly, Sadie answered.

"Hello?"

She heard sniffling on the other end of the line. "Sadie?"

She couldn't place the voice.

"Yes, this is Sadie? Who is this?"

More sniffling. "It's Ashleigh. You told me I could call you... if I needed help."

Shit.

Yes.

She had. And Gavin won the bet.

"Of course," Sadie yawned, swinging her legs to the side of the bed and stretching her back. "Are you okay? What's wrong?"

Ashleigh's sniffling increased to sobs. "I'm so sad. I miss him!"

"I'm sorry," Sadie said. "This is tough, what you're going through."

"And I don't know anyone here! I stayed home waiting for him all the time. I feel like a total loser."

"You're not," Sadie said. "You need a good night's sleep. Have you been sleeping?"

"No," Ashleigh cried. "I can't. What am I supposed to do next? Why am I even still here? I should leave town."

"If that's what you want to do," Sadie said. "Or—"

"Can you come over?" she asked. "I need to talk to someone. I'm so lonely."

Sadie suppressed a groan. She did not want to do that. On the list of things she wanted to do, that was very, very low on the list. And she was a little wary of Ashleigh. Could this be some sort of trap?

"Please," Ashleigh whined. "I need some company."

"Okay," Sadie relented. "Okay, I'll come over. Text me where you are, and I'll be there soon."

But Sadie wasn't going alone. She'd learned her lesson, multiple times, to not be anywhere near a potential murderer alone, for any reason. At all. Luckily, she had a sidekick sleeping in her guest bedroom.

A grumpy one. When she tapped on the door after struggling into clothes, he groaned at her. "Go away."

Sadie tapped again. "Aren't you here to be my protector?" she asked through the door.

More groaning, then the door opened a crack. "Do you need protecting?"

"Maybe? Kind of?"

His gaze sharpened. "Are you currently under threat?"

"Not at this exact moment, but I need to go see someone that's having a hard time, and I don't want to go alone."

Gavin shook his head. "Nope, I'm the house guy. Your other protector signed up for out-of-house duties."

Sadie frowned at him. "What?"

"Check the couch," he yawned. Then he shut the door in her face.

Confused, Sadie crept into the darkened living room, then jumped when a lump of blankets on the couch moved. She spotted a lock of golden hair and sighed, flipping on the living room light. "Merritt? How long have you been sleeping in my living room?"

* * *

He explained it to her on the short drive to the Mountain West Club, the luxury hotel where Ashleigh was staying in the penthouse suite.

"I stayed on the couch Wednesday night, too," he admitted. "Gavin knew. He was happy to have help in case something happened. I snuck out at six, before you woke up."

Sadie shook her head. "You should have told me."

"I didn't know if you'd want my help, and I was too worried about you not to stay. It's also not the first time I've done this, if you remember...though last time, your couches were much more comfortable."

"You can blame KitKat for that," Sadie grumbled. "I'm still not over it. When did you come in tonight?"

"Gavin let me in at eleven." He yawned.

"So, you've barely slept," Sadie said. "Some bodyguard you are."

"I've slept less under more threatening conditions," he assured her. "Now explain to me what we're doing?" He pulled into a street parking spot outside the hotel. Light snow was falling, having accumulated an inch or two overnight.

"Ashleigh called and said she's lonely and needs company. She sounded upset. She seems harmless to me? I don't know."

Merritt's jaw ticked. "I'm not sure about harmless." He pulled his phone out of his pocket, swiping around, then turning it for her to see. Sadie squinted at it. Great, she'd forgotten her glasses. He held it up so she could see better, and she finally just took it from him.

"Wah...?" Sadie tried to figure out what she was watching. It was a stage. A slim girl dressed vaguely like Katniss from *The Hunger Games* held a bow and arrow and danced around. She zoomed in on the video, looking at the girl's face. "Is that Ashleigh?"

"Yep," Merritt said grimly. "That's her Miss Teen USA talent program. Watch."

On the screen, Ashleigh did an interpretive dance with the bow, music swelling in the background. Then, when she was far stage left, she drew back her bow and fired...at a target on the other side of the stage, which exploded into a cloud of colorful, short-lived smoke. Sadie's jaw dropped. She did it again, and again, and again. And then danced her way to a final flourish, firing once more above her, and disappearing into the plume of rainbow smoke her shot produced.

"Wow," Sadie said. "That was amazing."

"And could be deadly."

Sadie considered it. "Wade wasn't killed with a bow and arrow."

"But she could have other training that makes her more likely to be able to kill someone with a pen. Do you know how hard that is? You have to really commit and use a lot of force."

Sadie blinked at him. "Do you have personal experience?" she squeaked.

"I've never done it," Merritt assured her. "At least not for real."

Sadie shrugged that off. Just more tantalizing bits of his life he revealed in little slivers that maybe, over time, would form a full picture.

"But you're missing something else," Merritt said. "The smoke."

"Right! The smoke bombs. Ooh. But...why?"

"That, I haven't worked out," Merritt admitted.

"Did you look up Madison's talent from when she was Miss Arizona?"

"Yeah, she's a singer. Nothing too exciting."

"Huh."

Sadie's phone buzzed in her hand. A text from Ashleigh.

r u here yet

Sadie sent her a quick yes back, and her and Merritt climbed out of the car. Sadie grabbed her bag out of the back-seat, and they headed in. The night clerk was waiting for them. He eyed Merritt suspiciously but let them into the elevator with his special key card, anyway.

"Top floor," he said, tapping the button, and the door closed, leaving Sadie and Merritt alone.

"Nice digs," Sadie said.

"Wouldn't expect anything less. I wonder how long he prepaid her stay."

Sadie grimaced. "I know. This girl needs a plan to get out of here."

But when Ashleigh answered their knock on her door, swinging it open and revealing the luxurious suite behind her, Sadie didn't blame her for not wanting to leave. The penthouse was multi-story, with floor-to-ceiling windows revealing the twinkling lights of town and the distant ski hill. It smelled of fresh flowers from the giant bouquet on the entryway table, and Sadie could just glimpse a gleaming full kitchen to the right. Looked like a pretty nice place to lie low, actually. She made herself focus on Ashleigh.

"Oh," the girl said in a small voice. "I didn't know you were bringing anyone."

Sadie patted Merritt's arm. "He insisted on coming out with me in the middle of the night. Safety first and all that." She held up the bag she brought. "But I brought some stuff. Face masks. Chocolate. Y'know, comfort stuff."

"That's nice," Ashleigh said, relenting. "At least I've met you before. Picnic buddies." She opened the door wide enough for them to come in, then shut and latched it behind them. "Come on in." She led the way into the large living room, which featured comfortable leather couches, the floor-to-ceiling windows, and a large TV tuned to a reality dating show. She slumped down onto the couch. The nearby table and rest of the couch were covered with blankets, balled up tissues and food containers. The mess had overtaken the kitchen, too, with more takeout containers piled on the island, broken-down cardboard boxes stacked next to the trash instead of being put out to be recycled. It was clear Ashleigh was having a hard time. Or she was really, really messy.

Sadie and Merritt sat on the other couch. It was awkwardly quiet for a minute, then Sadie broke the silence.

"What did you do today?"

Ashleigh snorted, gesturing around. "Literally this. I feel stuck. Where's my closure? He's dead, and I'm...invisible."

"Did you work on your podcast?"

Ashleigh shook her head. "It was a stupid idea. I don't know how to podcast, and if I started one, all I'd get were dudes complaining about my vocal fry."

Sadie dug around in the bag she'd brought, producing an empty notebook and a few gel pens. She put them on the table and pushed them over to Ashleigh. "Have you ever tried journaling? It can be a good way to think through your feelings."

Ashleigh sniffled. "That's sweet of you. I'll try it. But thanks for coming. I needed company."

"Do you have family you could call to come hang out with you?" Merritt asked.

Ashleigh shook her head. "They weren't exactly happy about my relationship with Wade. They never understood. I can't call them now, they'll just...gloat about it."

Sadie tried to remember back to when she'd been twenty years old. She'd been in college. There'd definitely been things her parents didn't understand. But she'd known, always, no matter what decisions she made, they would have her back, would welcome her back, no questions asked. She felt sympathy for Ashleigh that she didn't have the same sort of relationship with her own parents.

Ashleigh picked up her phone, scrolling. "And I called my sister. She has an apartment and a job, but she said I can't move in with her, even temporarily. So don't say I didn't try. I'm hanging out here, waiting for them to kick me out when I've overstayed whatever Wade paid, and crying. I don't know what else to do."

"Well, it's been three days," Sadie said gently. "You don't have to know what to do, yet. If you get kicked out here, I'm sure we could help you find a place to stay." Merritt stiffened next to her. She knew what he was thinking. If she wasn't careful, Ashleigh would end up staying at her house. And right now, she was his number one suspect for the smoke bombing incidents.

Ashleigh smiled at her weakly. "Thanks. I should ask, I guess. How long he prepaid for. That would give me a timeline and cut down my anxiety."

"It would," Sadie agreed.

"I will, in the morning, when the day manager's on." She picked up her phone again, scrolling through it. "It's just. I can't help but feel cheated. I don't even have text messages to scroll through." She hiccupped. "I can't mourn him by reliving our relationship. It's no fair!"

Sadie frowned. "Why...don't you have any messages?"

Ashleigh blinked at her. "Oh. You didn't know? Wade didn't have a phone. He was convinced 5G caused cancer or blah blah blah, I dunno, it was the most boomer thing about him. He never texted. He used a landline if he needed to call, or made someone else text me, like Elijah."

"I didn't know," Sadie said. She thought back to all the interactions she'd had with Wade, all the events she'd seen him at. And yeah. She couldn't remember him ever having a phone.

"But he didn't mind you having one?" Merritt asked.

"Oh, he hated it. When he was with me, I had to put it in a lockbox thing. I have like, no pictures either. He was so—" her voice broke. "So weird."

But Sadie had stopped paying attention. She heard Merritt say something to Ashleigh, but Sadie's gaze had caught on one of the boxes by the trash can. Only a few big, black letters were visible, but it was enough.

-OMBS. Ombs. B...ombs? Smoke bombs? There was a logo

on the box, too. If only she had her glasses! What brand had her dad pegged the smoke bombs as? Enola Gaye?

"Let me help you clean up," Sadie offered, thinking fast. "When I'm having a hard time, I struggle to clean." She stood, gathering the takeout containers off the coffee table. She carried them into the kitchen and put them on the counter. "Are the trash bags around here somewhere?" She started peeking into cabinets, under the sink.

Something in her voice must have cued Merritt because he got up to help, too.

"I think there's some in the hall pantry," Ashleigh said. She was scrolling on her phone, paying them little attention.

"Help me look?" She asked Merritt, who cocked an eyebrow at her questioningly. She made eyes at him, and they hustled into the hall. She opened the pantry door, both of them sticking their heads inside. "The box," she hissed at him. "I swear there's a—" she lowered her voice to be barely audible "—smoke bomb box out there by the trash."

Merritt's eyes widened. "Seriously?"

"Yes! You go check. Tell her you'll take the boxes out to be recycled, okay?"

Merritt nodded. "Okay, but I'm not leaving you."

That was a good idea. "I'll come up with a reason we both have to leave?"

Then they heard the footsteps behind them.

"That won't be necessary," Ashleigh said.

Chapter Twenty-One

Sadie and Merritt both turned, slowly. Sadie held her breath. She couldn't believe this. Ashleigh? Ashleigh had done all this?

Then she saw her. Tears poured down her face. She didn't hold a weapon. Her hands were in front of her, twisting anxiously. "I'll tell you," she sobbed. "I'll tell you everything."

Sadie and Merritt herded Ashleigh back into the living room. Sadie motioned for her to sit, but Merritt made them wait, pulling the blankets out and fluffing them, feeling around the edges of the cushions, before he let her sit back down. Ashleigh seemed oblivious, but Sadie knew what he was doing. Bodyguarding. Checking for weapons. Sadie was pretty sure Ashleigh didn't have any, though.

They all settled back in, and then Ashleigh began her story.

She really, really hated that Wade had run for Mayor. He'd been under enough scrutiny as a mayoral candidate that he'd barely been able to get away to see her for the last few months. And going out? Forget about it. They had to go out of town or risk being seen, and he couldn't leave town very often with campaign events all the time. And Ashleigh, who was absolutely *not* jealous of Madison, she promised, was sick of seeing the two of them out all the time in pictures. And while Wade had sworn up and down that as soon as the election was over, he'd divorce Madison so he could be with Ashleigh, Madison just looked too comfortable in all the pictures she saw.

But if he lost...

"I'm not dumb," Ashleigh declared. "I know I seem kind of dumb for all of this, but I'm not. I had a 4.0 in high school. I saw the polls, as few as they are in this Podunk town. The race might've been tight, but the locals in this town had no reason to vote for him. I loved him, but he had really terrible ideas."

"He did," Sadie agreed. "What do you think would've happened? If he'd lost?"

"I think he would've left Madison and stayed with me," Ashleigh said sadly. "That's why I did it. To make sure he would lose. Even though he was so convinced he would win. He'd say, 'I'll win, one way or another.' I never understood what he meant."

Sadie did. He'd planned to threaten Paige until she quit. With lies, or, as he'd resorted to, physical force.

"So, what did you do?" Sadie said. "We saw the box. We can help you if you just tell the truth."

"No one can help me," Ashleigh said bitterly. "I thought...I thought I would disrupt the voting. Maybe cause a lower turnout. Make sure he didn't get the votes."

"By doing what?" Merritt said, his voice stern. Sadie shot him a look. They were making progress. He didn't need to play bad cop.

"I swear we'll help you," Sadie said, her voice gentle. "I have a brilliant lawyer."

"When Wade moved me here, they packed my entire storage unit, and that included all my pageant stuff. I remembered I had a few leftover smoke devices...did you know that was my talent? I'm a killer archer, and I'd hit these exploding targets, then set off these smoke bombs with a remote. It was so cool. I never used the normal smoke color ones, though, so that's what I had left."

The smoke bombs would be pretty hard to trace. Ashleigh had competed in Miss Teen USA years ago. Who knows how long they'd been in her storage. Would she have gotten away with it if they hadn't seen the box?

"How did you do it?" Merritt asked.

"It was too easy," Ashleigh said. "They do open roller skating in that building on Sunday afternoons, and they keep the cones and stuff in the supply closet, so it's unlocked. I carried the device in my backpack, and when no one was watching, I skated in and set it up under a set of shelves."

"But how did you remote detonate it? That seems complicated."

Ashleigh shrugged. "I told you I wasn't dumb. I was on the robotics team. I set up a time detonator, so it was set to go off at a certain time. I didn't have to do anything after that." She gulped. "But then it all went wrong! It wasn't supposed to actually start a fire!"

"You said you put it under some shelves? Was it dusty back there?" Merritt asked.

"Yeah?"

"It wouldn't take much heat or spark to start a fire under shelves," Merritt said. "There could've been a mouse nest or something underneath there, too, or even in the walls. Plus, they could've stored chemicals, solvents, all kinds of things that would've helped a fire along with a spark. That's an old building."

Ashleigh paled. "It was completely an accident. And I had no idea it would provide cover for someone to murder him! I didn't know he was going there that morning! By the time I knew, based on a Facebook post from the campaign, it was too late for me to sneak in and deactivate it."

"So, you called in a bomb threat?" Sadie asked.

Ashleigh shook her head. "I texted it to 911 using an anonymous texting app while logged into the VPN I use to watch overseas Netflix."

Sadie thought back to the press conference. Had they specified it'd been called in? No. They'd said received. She'd assumed it'd been a phone call.

Merritt narrowed his eyes at Ashleigh. "That was pretty smart. They'll trace it eventually, though."

"But weren't you at the salon?" Sadie asked, remembering Ashleigh's alibi.

"I said I had to go to the bathroom," Ashleigh said. "But I was too late. I couldn't remember the exact time I'd set it for. I was too late." She collapsed into tears again, her head in her hands. Sadie watched her shoulders shake, then slid over to pat her back. Her and Merritt's eyes met.

"She didn't kill him," Sadie mouthed, and Merritt nodded his agreement. Sadie had been right that day at the press conference. This was two separate crimes. Or wait. Three! She abruptly stopped patting Ashleigh's back. "Wait! And then you smoke bombed my bakery? After I've been so nice to you?"

Ashleigh looked up, surprise on her face. "I dropped the last of them in a random dumpster. I didn't realize until I was at the end of the block that one of them had gone off, and then I ran! That was...your bakery? I'm so sorry! I didn't mean to. I was trying to get rid of the evidence without hurting anyone else. And I was so scared! It seems like no matter what I do, I make everything worse."

Sadie sighed. "I believe you. I don't know if I should, but I do."

"I do too," Merritt agreed. "And we'll help you. But...you

understand what you did, right? You interfered with a federal election. They're going to take this seriously."

Like *terrorism* seriously, Sadie thought to herself, but she didn't say it out loud. Ashleigh just cried harder. Sadie's heart hurt for her. She'd made a series of very, very poor decisions, and she was going to pay for them. On the other hand, she was only twenty years old. She'd have time to make changes in her life. But unfortunately, the next place Ashleigh was headed... was probably prison.

* * *

Nora was just as bubbly at five in the morning as any other time of day. She showed up with four coffees in a cardboard carrier and a bag of fresh bagels and cream cheese, which was impressive considering the bagel shop didn't open for another hour. Sadie shrugged off that mystery, though. They had a big enough one on their hands. There was still a killer on the loose.

Merritt and Sadie had convinced Ashleigh to shower while they cleaned up, so it was a squeaky-clean version of her that showed up at the kitchen island for coffee, a bagel, and a lawyer consultation. With no makeup on and her hair scraped back from her face in a wet braid, she looked even younger, and Sadie felt animosity for Wade bubble up in her again.

Ashleigh told her story to Nora and showed her the box.

Nora listened intently, asked a lot of questions, and then patted her hand. "I'm going to consult with another lawyer on this, and we're going to help you. I'll represent you, if you wish, pro bono. Do you understand what that means?"

"For free?" Ashleigh said, her voice quavering. "Why?"

"Because you're a good girl that got herself in a bad situation," Nora said. She leaned in closer. "Plus, us pageant girls need to stick together." She winked.

Merritt and Sadie left Ashleigh in Nora's capable, apparently-former-pageant-queen hands, with the promise to check in soon. They walked out of the lobby and onto the street into the dark. It was only six in the morning, and Sadie felt like she'd lived an entire day already. Snow had continued to fall while they were inside, a solid four inches now built up where the enterprising snow removal crews hadn't already shoveled. They paused under the awning, watching the snow.

"One mystery down," Merritt said. "That's better than the professionals have done."

"Yeah. And my best friend's in *jail*. It's not good enough. I need to figure out who killed Wade."

"Well, that's what the summit's for, right? Maybe with the smoke bombs out of the picture, we'll be able to uncover the truth if we all put our heads together."

"I hope so," Sadie sighed. Kendall had scheduled their reservation for nine in the morning, so she had three hours to kill until then. "Take me home? I might as well spend the next few hours sleeping."

"C'mon, sleepyhead," Merritt said. "I'll take ya."

Chapter Twenty-Two

But Tyrone wasn't in the mood. He let her crawl back into bed, let her doze for an hour, and then insisted it was time for a walk. Which meant her bodyguards were out, because Tyrone hadn't insisted *she* take him for a stroll in days.

Sighing, Sadie rolled out of bed, being careful of her arm. It didn't hurt as bad today, which she was grateful for. In fact, she was going to skip the morning pain pill and take ibuprofen instead. Progress. After struggling into long underwear, a half-zip base layer top that barely stretched over the cast, wool socks, and snow bibs, she checked the living areas. Empty. A note from Merritt on the kitchen island said he'd run home to shower and would be back at eight-thirty to take her to the summit. She glanced at the apple clock. Not her smartwatch, which she must not have put on the charger correctly overnight because it was dead, but the actual red apple clock on the kitchen wall. Seven-forty-five. Just enough time to take Tyrone for a brisk one, and then come home and change.

She put on her boots and coat and dressed Tyrone in his

reflective jacket. It was light outside, but it never hurt, especially with the snow.

Right before she left, she turned back, using the pen on the counter to add her own note underneath Merritt's.

Taking Tyrone for a walk. Should be back by 8:15ish.

See? Progress. Telling someone where she was going instead of heading out on her own. She was proud of herself.

It wasn't until she was a few blocks from home that she realized she'd forgotten her phone.

Maybe not progress, then.

But it was a great day for a walk. The snow was falling gently, a lightweight, airy snow that didn't get her jacket wet. Many of the sidewalks had been shoveled, so the going was pretty easy, and she'd put traction grips on her boots just in case. Her orthopedist had emphasized, again and again, that she needed to be careful while her arm was healing. Falling and breaking it again would almost surely result in surgery, and that sounded awful. She liked being two days into the four-week cast period. She'd be rolling out dough again by Christmas...which was important. She had a lot of sugar cookies to make.

Tyrone loved the snow, regularly flopping down on his back to roll in it or putting his nose down to tunnel through it until it built up over his head and he burst through at a jog that would pull Sadie after him. She scolded him but laughed. It felt good to get her blood pumping. Maybe it would get her brain turning, too, just in time for the summit.

It must have worked because that's when she thought of it.

She was replaying the conversation they'd had with Ashleigh in her mind and marveling over the ability for a modern person live smartphone-free. Aside from the weird beliefs he had about 5G or radio waves, the general inconvenience that must have caused not only for him, but for everyone in his circle! She snorted, and Tyrone snorted too, though he did because he got snow in his nose. She supposed billionaires could inconvenience everyone around them if they paid enough.

And Madison had a phone. Had he made her lock it up in a special lockbox in their house? Had the 5G fears extended to not having Wi-Fi? How did Madison entertain herself without Netflix? Madison had even been using her phone that day at the polling place. She'd seen her scrolling on it in line and...

And.

Madison had been on the phone when Sadie stumbled out of the building.

Their eyes had met.

And Sadie had been able to make out the words she was yelling into the phone. "Pick up! Pick up!"

She'd thought Madison was calling Wade.

But Wade didn't have a phone.

Wade *didn't have a phone.*

So, who was she calling?

Who would she call in the worst moment of her life?

The answer, it turned out, was right in front of her.

Tyrone pulled on the leash, leaving the sidewalk to sniff around a sign in the yard of a tidy brick house that'd been converted to offices. He lifted his leg on the sign, tail wagging, and Sadie's eyes widened as she read the words on it: William Pierce, Esq.

"Called me right away, so panicked. So upset," he'd said yesterday. That's who she'd been calling. Not her husband. Her lawyer. *Their* lawyer. Her mind raced.

Tyrone lowered his leg, sniffing the air, then quirked his head to the side, listening. He turned to look at her and barked.

And then Sadie heard it, too.

The yelling. A shrill woman's voice, and a harried man's. Madison Fisher was meeting with her lawyer. And she wasn't happy.

* * *

Sadie snuck up the walkway to the building. The yelling was coming from the front room, and the curtains were open. The two of them were inside, Madison standing in front of the desk, Billy cowering behind it.

"Tell me!" Madison screamed.

Sadie hid behind a snow-covered shrub, shortening the leash to keep Tyrone out of sight, too. Why was Billy cowering? She strained to see, her glasses fogging up from her breaths panting in and out.

"Tell me who he left it to," Madison yelled again.

"I can't, I can't," Billy begged. "Please don't hurt me. I didn't want to tell you! You didn't deserve this!"

Hurt him? Sadie peered around the bush, then gasped. Madison had a gun aimed at him. A small pistol, something she could've easily hidden in her purse. And she did not look good. Her normally smooth hair was a tangled mess around her head. She swayed on her feet, like she was exhausted, or drunk. Her eyes were red and bloodshot, tears streaming down her face. She rubbed her sleeve over her eyes to clear the tears, then put both hands on the gun, trying to steady it.

"I will shoot you!"

"No, you won't," Billy said placatingly. "You don't have this in you. I know you're upset about Wade, but this is making it worse. Maybe I can help you find someone to challenge the will!"

"Don't patronize me," Madison said, her voice bitter. "You

wouldn't have written him a will that could be challenged. You were in on this with him! You deserve to die. Just like he did."

Sadie gasped, then ducked back behind the tree. *Shit!* Had they heard her? Did that mean Madison had killed Wade?

Tyrone leaned heavily against her, looking up at her worriedly. This was bad. Sadie looked around the neighborhood, hoping to see someone walking by, but the street was deserted. Should she sneak away to find help for Billy? How could she have forgotten her phone? She didn't even know what time it was. Was it past the time she'd written in her note? Would Merritt come looking for her? It wasn't like he could follow their footsteps, not with the sidewalks mostly cleared.

No, no one was coming to look for her.

And no one was coming to help Billy.

So, she should.

She took a deep breath, then peered around the bush again. They were still arguing with one another. She felt the leash tighten, Tyrone straining on it, and looked down at him. In the blink of an eye, she saw what he was looking at and tried to stop him, but it was useless.

Tyrone loved squirrels. Some time ago, he'd made friends with one that had nested in her chimney. For all Sadie knew, that was his since-evicted chimney friend.

He barked, loud and happy, a hello.

And then the shot rang out.

Desperate to get away, knowing her cover was blown, not knowing if the shot had been aimed at her—though the window hadn't broken, so?—Sadie loosed the leash, taking one step, then another away from the window. Then Tyrone lunged to chase the squirrel, and she lost her hold on the leash and lost her balance. She fell forward, slipping in the snow, trying to twist to land on her back and not her bad arm, and mostly succeeded, but the jostling sent pain jolting through her arm and up into her shoulder and back. She clutched at it, groaning, knowing she needed to get up, to crawl away. "Tyrone," she moaned. She lifted her head, but he was gone. Her heart leaped in fear. "Tyrone?"

She heard footsteps in the snow and turned her head, hoping to see him running to her, but it wasn't Tyrone.

It was Madison Fisher.

"Your dog ran off," she said. "You know what I have in my pocket, right?" She had her right hand in her pocket, and there was a hard angle visible from the outside. Sadie knew.

"I do," Sadie said.

"Then get up and get inside. Or I'll kill you, too."

Chapter Twenty-Three

Madison had shot Billy.

Actually shot him. But he wasn't dead.

He had a wound on his arm, but Sadie wasn't sure if that was purposeful or poor aim. Either way, when she walked into the office, Madison gripping her good arm tightly, she gasped. "You shot him!"

"And I'll shoot you, too," Madison threatened, pushing her toward him. "Stay over there."

Sadie stumbled, trying again not to fall, then steadied herself and sank down against the wall. Billy was sprawled on his back, blood seeping from his left arm. He was trying to staunch the flow with his hand. His eyes met hers, frantic.

"Didn't take it well, did she?" Sadie whispered to him, and his eyes bugged out. Apparently, it wasn't time for jokes.

"I'm going to help him stop the bleeding on his arm," Sadie announced to Madison, who was snapping the curtains on the window closed, still watching them, right hand in her pocket.

"Fine," Madison bit out. She stomped to the sideboard, pouring herself a generous portion of whiskey and muttering to herself. She tipped it back.

Sadie took off her coat, folding it so the absorbent, soft side was out, then checked the wound on Billy's arm. It was clean through, which was probably good news? It was bleeding, but not pumping blood out, so that was also good news. Sadie arranged the coat so it covered the back and front of the wound and pressed down.

Billy moaned, his eyes fluttering.

"Don't pass out on me, Billy," Sadie said. "Stay awake. I have to hold pressure to stop the bleeding."

"Of course you know him," Madison said accusingly. "You're such a nosy bitch!"

"I've actually heard that before," Sadie said with more confidence than she felt. "Listen, why don't you run for it? Leave, and I'll give you a five-minute head start before I call for help."

Billy grunted his dissent, but Sadie didn't look at him. Of course she'd call for help right away if Madison ran.

"Why? Why bother?" Madison slammed the empty glass down on the desk. "How dare that bastard give me *nothing?*"

"I agree," Sadie said. "You supported him all those years, you deserve his estate. Or part of it."

"All of it," Madison said, her eyes flashing. "I gave that man my entire youth, and he replaced me with a younger version of me. How dare he!"

"He was a right bastard," Sadie said, her tone even. "You don't need to ruin your life because of it."

Madison narrowed her eyes. "You think you're helping, don't you? Such a helpful girl. Such a helpful friend. Ugh. You make me sick. Always tagging along with Miss Gates-Ortiz," she said snidely. "Pathetic. Though, in the end, Paige helped me out. Everything lined up, you see? It was like...it all came together in front of me, all the pieces, and it worked perfectly. It was a thing of beauty."

"What do you mean?" Sadie asked, her mouth dry. She

glanced at Billy, whose eyes were still open, watching Madison warily.

"You still don't get it, do you? I killed him! And I framed that bitch. In like, no time."

Sadie gaped at her. To hear her admit it out loud shocked her. "How?" Sadie asked. "I was there. I don't understand how you did it."

"You want me to do the thing where the villain recounts their crimes for the audience? Well guess what. There is no audience. I don't have to put on a show. Billy needs to tell me what I need to know, and then I'll leave. It's that easy."

Sadie looked at Billy. "Tell her?"

He closed his eyes, breathing shallowly. Then opened them. He wet his lips. "He left his estate to his mother, Elijah, and a couple kids you don't know about from his twenties. And Ashleigh." He looked at Sadie pleadingly. Like she could save him from Madison's wrath. She was already doing everything she could to keep him alive. She had one working arm. What else could she do? How could she help?

Madison stepped closer, her mouth agape. "Children? He had *children* and never told me?"

"He wasn't in their lives, at all, ever," Billy said. "He paid the mothers off back then. But he decided...a few months ago... to put them in the will."

"And he took me out?" she screeched.

"Oh, Madison," Billy sighed. "You were never in it."

"And Ashleigh was?" She pulled the gun out, waving it around wildly. "That whore?" She spit.

"Please," Sadie said, her tone still even despite her fear. "Please. He told you the information. Please just go. There's nothing to be done about it right now. We won't call anyone, you can run. Get in your car and go."

Madison laughed bitterly. "There's nowhere to go. I should

end it. For all of us." Her gaze flickered to the gun in her hand. "I have enough bullets, I think." She pointed it at Billy. "One." Sadie. "Two." Herself. "Three. Heck, I even have a couple extra, just in case. Maybe I should wait to see if anyone comes after you, use them on them."

Sadie fought rising panic. She'd thought Madison was a wronged wife out for revenge, but maybe. Maybe she was an actual madwoman. How could she get them out of this? Her gaze bounced around the room, looking for something, anything to help them. Her and Billy were up against the wall. There was a bookcase recessed into it, full of heavy books. Okay. She could throw a heavy book. She'd have to reach across Billy, though. There was the chair. Could she shove it at her, knock her over somehow? And that was it. Damnit, Billy. No fireplace with a convenient poker nearby?

Madison was pacing now, her eyes never leaving them as she muttered to herself. Time was ticking by. Ah. Time. There was at least a clock in the room. Of course—a lawyer charged by the six-minute increment. It was 8:27 A.M. She was twelve minutes late. Was Merritt out looking for her? Where was Tyrone? Her heart beat fast. He was a good dog. He would stay out of the street, right? Hopefully someone had picked up his leash and taken him home. That would be a sign that something was wrong. People could be searching for her already. And maybe someone else had heard the gunshot? But that'd been ten minutes ago, at least. The police would've been here by now.

"I want to know how you did it," Sadie said, trying to buy time. "When I came out of the voting booth, where were you?"

Madison made a disgusted noise. "You're so damned curious. Fine. I'll tell you. Before I kill you, ha! Okay. Here's what happened. On the way to the polling place, Wade told me," her voice broke. "He told me he was leaving me. He was annoyed with me, so he decided then was the time to tell me. And I knew. I knew if he left me, I got nothing. I was so upset. It was good I got told to zip up my coat because I was shivering, from cold and shock. I still had my gloves on, the whole time."

Sadie remembered. She remembered Madison wearing gloves inside but seeing the glint of Madison's ring in the sunshine when she'd walked outside. She'd taken off her gloves after. Probably because they were covered in blood.

"My hands were shaking. I was in shock. He'd...he'd never been a nice man, but I thought he appreciated what I did for him. How I made his life easier. I did so much for him. I even overlooked Ashleigh. I never thought he would leave me for her. I thought I knew. I thought he was smart enough to know it would look bad for him to be with someone so young."

Sadie remembered hearing them talk in line behind her, remembered thinking they were not happy but not hearing exactly why.

"When we went into the booths, I stared at the ballot. I didn't want to vote for him. Then the alarm sounded. I stepped out, and he'd taken off. Without me. His beloved wife," she said bitterly. "I watched him grab Paige, threaten her. She... that wily bitch. She slipped out of her coat to get away from him. I watched it fall to the ground. And something else fell out of her hand. She ran off, and he turned around and saw me watching. Something in my eyes must have told him...because he started backing away from me. The smoke was billowing, it was getting hard to see. I looked around. We were alone. I reached down and picked up the coat, and the other thing. A pen. A beautiful, expensive Montblanc. And that idiot. He watched me as I walked up to him. Stalked him. I held the coat up, and he looked confused. He yelled, and then I jammed that pen into his neck and pushed him over. His head smacked hard on the cement. I knew he was dead. The blood...spurted everywhere, but I wiped it off with Paige's coat. No one noticed the red bits on my red jacket. I found some drops in my hair later, but...no one noticed. I cried too much for them to look too closely. I was the perfect wife, refusing to move, waiting for her husband to come out, collapsing when he did so, dead."

Sadie felt sick.

"I tossed the jacket into the smokiest part of the room, hoping it would burn up, and then put my gloves in my pockets and went outside. No one noticed me slip out. They were all busy looking for you."

Her eyes focused on Sadie. "And you've been driving me crazy ever since. Showing up at the memorial. How dare you! It was supposed to be my moment. The grieving widow, receiving condolences. You know, I've heard about candidates dying while on the ballot and being elected, and their wives serving for them. I thought maybe...maybe I'd be mayor. I'd worked hard enough. I deserved something. But I think I would have turned it down. I wanted my money, and then I was getting out of this frozen hellhole and going somewhere warm. Not Arizona. Hawaii. Tahiti. Tropical. And then Ashleigh was there! She's so dumb! And now...she's getting his money and I'm not." Madison shook her head. "How did it all go so wrong?"

She put her shoulders back. "But I know how to fix it." She looked at Sadie sadly. Then turned the gun on herself.

"No!" Sadie shouted. She reached across Billy, grabbing the heaviest book she could lift, and threw it at Madison. It struck her in the stomach, and she stumbled, the gun clattering across the room. Sadie grabbed another one, throwing it at Madison's head this time. It hit her, and she fell to the floor, moaning. Sadie crawled over, her arm screaming in pain. She needed to incapacitate her. Tie her up. Hold her hands. Something.

Madison was awake, looking around for the gun. So, Sadie did the only thing she could think of.

What had Kendall said Baxter did when Sully got hit in the face with a pool cue? He sat on the perpetrator.

So, she sat on her.

"Oof," Madison grunted. Sadie scrabbled for Madison's hands, grabbing one with her good hand, then putting her legs over the other.

"Just stay still," Sadie warned, panting. "For the love of everything, Billy, tell me you can get up and call the police."

He moaned from the floor. She wasn't out of this yet. If he couldn't call the police, she wasn't sure how long she could hold Madison. She'd gone limp, but was she only pretending? Was she trying to get Sadie to relax so she could throw her off? Sadie outweighed her by at least a hundred pounds, but still. Madison had two working arms and the rage of a jilted, written-out-of-the-will wife.

Then something caught her eye out the window. There was still a crack in the curtains. And through it, she could see red and blue lights.

Thank goodness.

A minute later, she heard the front door banging open, then footsteps in the hall. The office door opened, and Agent Cooke appeared behind a windbreaker-wearing, gun-brandishing agent.

Sadie relaxed marginally.

"Oh, Alice," she said. "Good. You're here. But I've already thrown the book at her."

Chapter Twenty-Four

There were questions. So many questions.

Sadie's first, after she'd informed the agents in the room where the gun was, that Billy had a gunshot wound, and she needed help to contain Madison, was if Tyrone was okay.

"Okay?" Agent Cooke had asked, flabbergasted. "He's the hero of the day! That dog brought us here!"

Sadie supposed she could forgive him for the squirrel incident, in that case. She was reunited with him outside, where Merritt held his leash, worry creasing his face. When he saw her, whole, if a little rumpled and sweaty, the relief was palpable. She walked directly into his arms, and didn't leave them, except to hug and love on Tyrone, for a long time.

Billy was rolled out on a stretcher. He caught her eye as they loaded him up, waving at her gratefully. "I owe you one," he mouthed, miming drinking a beer, and Sadie gave him a thumbs up.

Madison was led out in handcuffs. She glared darkly at Sadie as she walked by, and Sadie was pretty sure she heard her mutter, "fat bitch."

Which made Sadie smile. Because Sadie being fat had saved them all. She'd have to thank Bax for the idea later.

And when all the questions were answered, and they could finally go home, Sadie and Merritt chose to walk back. Hand in hand. Well, hand in hand, and leash in hand. Good thing Merritt had two working ones.

* * *

Two Weeks Later

"I never thought I'd see my name in lights," Kamari whispered to Sadie, and Sadie squeezed her arm.

"I knew we would," she said.

"Hell yeah!" Kendall yelled. "Let's get a selfie!"

It took a minute, but they eventually got everyone in the picture, thanks to Max's long arms.

There was Max and Sage, and Sadie and Merritt, and Kamari and Kendall, and Claire and Bax and Sully, and Nash and Jorge, and Robin and Arlo, and, to everyone's eternal delight, Mayor-Elect Paige Gates-Ortiz and her beautiful family.

They were all there for Kamari's big debut. The bad things were behind them, and the future was as bright as Kamari's name on the theater marquee.

WHITE OUT starring KAMARI ROBINSON, it declared. Along with some other big names in the freeride world, but none of them were as important as hers, at least to Jackson Hole. This was the global premiere. Soon, Kamari would be jetting around—well, flying business class, at least—to help promote it at screenings and outdoor film festivals across the country. Between that and the freeride circuit she'd qualified for, they wouldn't be seeing much of Kamari this winter. But they could miss her another day.

Today they would celebrate her.

After a dozen photos of her in front of the marquee, and the movie poster, and a TikTok or two, including extra footage for later, they entered the theater. Kamari and the other athletes attending had a roped off balcony VIP section, so they filtered into it. Excitement buzzed throughout the theater. Music pumped through speakers. The local junior ski team, particularly starry-eyed because Kamari was one of their coaches and she was *in the movie*, was selling 50/50 raffle tickets. Merritt bought ten arm lengths. Sadie hoped he won, because it was guaranteed he'd donate his half of the pot, too.

They had time until the movie started, so beverages were acquired, and everyone settled in to visit. It'd been a busy couple of weeks since that morning at Billy Pierce's law office.

Moose's had reopened. Sadie was grateful no actual damage had been done aside from a couple days of lost profits.

Gavin had held his soft launch of Multitudes, and tonight was their very first real service. They were all banned from stepping foot near the building for a week, at least. Sadie couldn't wait to see it running at full force.

Kendall and Claire had set a wedding date for the spring.

Billy Pierce was recovering fine and had decided to retire from law. The last Sadie heard from him, he was considering moving abroad with the proceeds of his condo sale. She wished him the best.

Tyrone was going through an intensive no-barking-at-squirrels-or-deer training at Hoback Hounds after his one tiny indiscretion almost led to his mother being killed. But he'd also received the "Dog Bone to the City" for being a hero, so really a mixed bag for him. What Sadie knew was that he was absolutely the bestest, goodest boy, no matter what.

Max and Sage had moved in together, which meant Sadie had an empty basement once Kamari took off on her tour. That hadn't happened in a long, long time.

The Wilson bakery kitchen—they'd taken to calling it Moose's West—was finished, and Sadie was deep into recruiting new talent to expand the business. Maybe the basement wouldn't be empty for long.

Sully had managed to injure his eye in a skiing accident and was wearing an eyepatch for a few weeks. Sadie thought it became him.

Baxter had a girlfriend but wouldn't tell anyone who it was. Kendall was on the case, which meant they'd all known soon.

Not to be left out, Jorge had gone on a date with Mrs. Wright, the city clerk. He refused to talk about it, but whenever anyone asked, his cheeks got red.

Nancy Fisher had taken her photos to every news outlet, and not one had published the photos of Merritt, Nora, and Paige. The official announcement of the development Gotham Enterprises was working on was coming soon.

Nash had hosted the annual tapping of the winter keg at the brewery, and Sadie and Merritt had attended together. Almost... like a date. Though neither of them had said anything about it.

She'd asked Merritt a few important questions.

Yes, he was no longer employed by the government. No, he would not specify why. He was living in a short-term rental in South Jackson for now. And yes. He was back. For good.

Robin and Arlo had made a big decision. They were staying. For the winter, and maybe for good. Though they didn't plan on settling too much, they were in the market for the ultimate vanlife rig, and planning on traveling six months out of the year. Sadie was thrilled for them.

In more big news, Will Nolan was leaving town, headed

back to Washington state to be closer to his son. She hoped she saw him, one more time, before he left town. To say goodbye, and good luck. She wondered who would replace him. Hopefully she'd never need to find out.

And the Gates-Ortiz family was healing. Paige had been released from holding the same day Madison had gone in, all charges dropped. There was no apology for her. A week later, they'd sat on Sadie's back deck with hot cocoas laced with peppermint schnapps and cried together. But they'd toasted to the future, whatever it might hold.

At the next town council meeting, Paige had planned to resign. But when she took her seat, she'd found the entire room, and the overflow room, and the hallway, and the snow-covered front lawn of town hall, filled with people asking her not to. Asking her to serve, the way they'd elected her to do. Even her usual opponents on the council had voiced their support. She'd be sworn in as Mayor after the first of the year. She'd already commissioned matching pantsuits for her and Luna for the ceremony.

Ashleigh had taken a deal negotiated by the delightful Nora. She was going to be incarcerated for some time, but she'd decided to get her college degree while she was in. Max talked to her regularly, and Sadie couldn't think of anyone better to mentor the girl through her time inside. Ashleigh was still grappling with the inheritance she'd received from Wade. Some of it would pay her ordered restitution, but there would still be a chunk of money when she came out. She'd started talking to her parents again, and Sadie hoped that relationship would heal.

Madison had not taken a deal, which meant there would be some difficult times ahead with a trial for Sadie and everyone else that would need to testify. Investigators had found additional evidence once pointed toward the actual perpetrator.

Madison had attempted to dispose of her bloody red coat and gloves, but they'd found it at the transfer station after what Sadie could imagine was a messy search. Her full confession to Sadie with a still-conscious-but-barely Billy in the room was also another nail in the coffin. Sadie tried not to think about Madison much.

The investigators had left town, the fairgrounds were open and being rehabbed. Sadie had even gotten her car back, though she still couldn't drive it one-armed. The national news cycle had moved on, too, even if it would take the town a while to get over it.

Sadie's arm was doing okay. She was sick of her cast, and it itched, but she was more than halfway through getting it off. She couldn't wait. She missed rolling dough, a task she thought she'd never miss.

"Kamari!" The call was simultaneous, from a group. They all dangled over the balcony rail, searching for where it was coming from. Sadie spotted them first.

"Ohmygod!" She pointed. It was the Table of Regulars. Wait. She squinted at them. Were they...?

"Are they naked?" Kendall squeaked.

"No," Sadie said, figuring it out. She laughed. "They're wearing shirts that make them look like they're naked, but they've painted Kamari's name on themselves. Six letters...plus an exclamation point!"

"I worship them," Kendall said, her voice awed.

"I can't decide if that's embarrassing or not," Kamari said, deadpan. But Sadie saw the twinkle of a tear in her eye. She waved at them, then blew them a bunch of kisses. Millie Yin pretended to faint when she caught hers.

At least Sadie hoped she pretended.

Then the film was starting.

They all took their seats.

Kamari was in the opening reel, and the theater exploded in applause for their hometown girl. The standing ovation lasted so long the theater actually paused the movie. Sadie didn't know they could do that. Kamari finally stood to wave, and gestured for the other performers to stand, too.

Finally, everyone settled, and the film started again.

Merritt sat on Sadie's right. So they could hold hands. They hadn't taken it any further than that, and Sadie didn't know what was happening between them, exactly. She just knew it felt good, watching Kamari absolutely destroy the gnar on the screen, her hand in Merritt's, surrounded by her loved ones. It felt like the way things were supposed to be. They would have time to figure out the details later. That was another chapter.

Another story.

* * *

Sadie and the gang investigate a mountain town tradition gone wrong in SANTA DROP MURDER, releasing 11/7/2023 and available now to preorder on Amazon at https://amzn.to/3I7IxAZ!

* * *

Want a free short story featuring the Moose's Bakery crew? Check out all my interstitial shorts at https://suepepperauthor.com/cozy-mystery-books/

* * *

Sign up for my newsletter to always be in the know at https://suepepperauthor.com/stay-in-touch/

Sue Pepper

* * *

Thank you for reading! If you liked this book, please leave a review on Amazon, Goodreads, BookBub, or wherever you leave reviews. It's the best way to help more readers find this series, and more readers means I can write more books!

Author's Note

I mention a lot of amazing women in this book: Ruth Bader Ginsburg, Elizabeth Warren, Alexandria Ocasio-Cortez, Kamala Harris, Jeanette Rankin, Gabby Giffords, Cori Bush, Nancy Pelosi, Shirley Chisholm. This is a completely non-inclusive list of women I admire for making the world a better place, smashing glass ceilings, and being badasses. Want to support more women in politics? Check out the Vote Mama Foundation, Emily's List, Run for Something, or your own local races.

As far as I know, the Teton County Fairgrounds haven't been used as polling place, at least recently, but they were front and center in my mind when I wrote this book thanks to the renewed discourse surrounding their future. That will be a story to watch.

The as-yet-named brewery in this book is inspired by Snake River Brewing Co., my family's favorite weekend hang out. If you're in the area, stop by for the buffalo cauliflower special, an Earned It IPA, and lawn games in the summer/fire pit in the winter. It's worth it. I don't think there's a scruffy redhead behind the bar named Nash, but you never know.

When I imagined the Coop, the not-dive-bar featuring the at-least-once-annulled bartender friend of Kendall's, Jack, I had The Bird in mind. The view from their deck is spectacular, though I don't think they have mozzarella sticks on their menu.

Jackson Hole is in the midst of a housing crisis. Many, many people, including my family, have been forced out of the community because of income inequality, a lack of affordable housing, and encroaching billionaires. I am donating a portion of the profits from this series to ShelterJH, an organization building grassroots and political power in Jackson Hole so that all community members can live where they work. I encourage you to give them your support and read through their policy platform. They have much better ideas on how to fix the problem than my works of fiction provide.

You might not know this, but authors can't quote song lyrics in their stories due to copyright laws. Which is a problem for me, who thinks mostly in song lyrics. I get around this by telling you the song I'm thinking of, but if you want more behind the scenes looks at what I *would have* written if I could, as well as Moose's Bakery discourse and special fan-only sneak peeks, join my Facebook Group, the Moose's Bakery Table of Regulars.

Acknowledgments

Every time I sit down to write my acknowledgments, I squirm in my seat and procrastinate. You've never seen my kitchen cleaner than when I'm supposed to be writing acknowledgments. Not because I'm not thankful, but because I'm so overwhelmingly thankful for the love and support in my life I don't know where to start.

So, while my dishwasher runs and I resist scrubbing the baseboards, here we go:

To my husband, who reached a career goal while I was head down in this book: I'm so proud of you. I call you a real-life action hero in my author bio, and you prove it day in and day out at work and at home. I love you. Plus, you're hot af, as Kendall would say.

To my kids: this book is for you. I'm waiting with bated breath to see what you do with this world. I know you're going to rock it. Also, I'm saving bail money and making friends with lawyers, for all the good trouble you'll get in.

Thank you to my amazing beta readers, Lea and Jen. Thanks for loving the Moose's Crew! Readers should thank Lea, too—the amount of book ideas I get from her means I'll be writing this series for ages. And thanks to Jen for finally getting it through my head how to use the correct pronoun in the subject when there are two subjects. Readers should probably thank her, too, for making me more readable.

Thanks to my Top Chef friends, Rachael, Kristen, and

Leah. I finished this book just in time for our busy season. We're like accountants!

Thanks to Amber, June, Jen, and Audra, the LV Friends Mastermind. We're accomplishing great things, and I'm so glad we're doing it together.

Thanks to my Sisters in Crime Columbia River Chapter. Our weekly write-ins keep me going and our monthly meetings inspire me.

To H, who inspired me to write Paige and her journey.

Lastly, thank you to my readers. Who knew there was an audience for cursy cozies that explicitly despise billionaires? Y'all are my people, and I'll write for you forever, promise. 🤍

About the Author

Sue Pepper writes not so cozy mysteries in the Pacific Northwest where she lives with her two kids, elderly dachshund, and real-life action hero husband. A former resident of Jackson Hole, Wyoming pushed out by the billionaire-caused housing crisis, she enjoys writing revenge and redemption for the fictional residents of her Jackson Hole Moose's Bakery Not So Cozy Mystery series, starting with her debut, Mountain Town Murder.

Find her online at www.suepepperauthor.com, Amazon, BookBub, Goodreads, Facebook, TikTok, and Instagram.

Also by Sue Pepper

Jackson Hole Moose's Bakery Not So Cozy Mystery Series

Available in print wherever books are sold, and in eBook on Amazon and Kindle Unlimited:

Mountain Town Murder, #1

Hot Springs Murder, #2

Boss Babe Murder, #3

Tourist Trap Murder, #4

Election Day Murder, #5

Santa Drop Murder, #6 — preorder now, publishing 11/7/2023

FREE interstitial short stories available at www. suepepperauthor.com/books:

Sadie Moose and a Recipe for Disaster, #0.5 — available in the *Riddles, Resolutions, and Revenge* anthology

Sadie Moose and the Escape from the North Pole, #1.5

Sadie Moose and a Deadly Secret Admirer, #2.5

Sadie Moose and a Patchwork of Peril, #3.5

Sadie Moose and the Ruff Day, #4.5

www.ingramcontent.com/pod-product-compliance
Lightning Source LLC
Chambersburg PA
CBHW021352150726
47989CB00005B/2218